ONE LAST STRIKE

BEFORE DARK

A Story

Ron Rhody

Outer Banks Publishing Group
Raleigh/Outer Banks

www.outerbankspublishing.com

info@outerbankspublishing.com

This book is a work of fiction.

FIRST EDITION – March 2021

Library of Congress Control Number: 2021933264

ISBN 13 - 978-1-7341687-9-2
eISBN – 978-1-0057135-6-0

FOR

Monk Hudson, Don Wheeler, Bob Regan, and
Dee Chambliss
... they were worth the price of admission

O Karma, Dharma, pudding & pie,
Gimme a break before I die:
Grant me wisdom, will & wit,
purity, probity, pluck, & grit.
Trustworthy, loyal, helpful, kind,
gimme great abs & a steel-trap mind.
Make the bad people good--
and the good people nice;
And before our world goes over the brink,
teach the believers how to think.

Philip Appleman
With apologies for the tinkering

Acknowledgements

Roe Rogers, Russ Hatter, Alice Irby, my brother Don Rhody, and, most particularly, Jane Hobson Snyder, helped make this book one in which I have to admit I do take a bit of pride. A good story well told permits it. If you will forgive the immodesty, this book, is that – a good story, well told.

Roe, Russ, Donnie, and Alice were early readers. Their reactions and critique were invaluable.

Jane proofed and edited the book, not only enriching the way the story is told, but the caliber of the story itself.

Brad Beard designed the cover, catching the mood and the nuance of the story beautifully.

My thanks to one and all.

PREFACE

Sunday, September 16

He's just made the turn onto the narrow country road that runs along the creek and will take him to the cottage.

A little after midnight. No moon.

The stars obscured by scudding clouds.

He has the driver-side window down, feels the moisture in the air. Thinks, rain coming. Thinks… I'm gonna die.

OK. Alright.

No surprise. We all are.

But … me?

A month?

He rolls up the window, twists on the wiper, slows down. He's had a little more to drink than he should have, doesn't want to end the night in a ditch. The rain has come, a light misty rain.

Feeling sorry for yourself, ole buddy?

Damn right.

All alone on a tenebrous night and the Grim Reaper out there in the shadows.

Tenebrous?

Aw, come on. Find something up-tempo. A little Freddie. Some Madonna maybe. Hell, even Elton. You're on home ground. Friends at beck and call. Snap out of it.

SATURDAY, SEPTEMBER 8
Day One

The Wyoming sky is so vast and cloudless he thinks he could see forever if only the light would last.

Below, a solitary figure is silhouetted against the river. In the twilight, the surface is as flat as glass. In this whole great sweep of land and sky there is no one else. Just the lone fisherman against the sheen of the water, making graceful casts, trying for one last strike before dark.

Jordan is standing on the porch at the lodge sipping bourbon and searching for the first star. The feel of night coming on and the taste of the bourbon flicks his memory. He was what, sixteen? After that first hunt, standing in the circle of men around the truck at the edge of the cornfield, dry stalks rustling in the breeze, the last dove of the day darting into the night, the flask passed to him—like he was one of them? Lord, that was sweet.

Ah, well.

That morning on the phone with Danny: "Tell me my options."

"There are no options. You have an inoperable intracranial aneurism, a brain aneurism. When it bursts, you'll die."

"What are the odds?'

"That it will burst? Short of a miracle, dead certain. You'll see a blinding light or feel like you've been hit in the head with a baseball bat, a pain more intense than you have ever felt. Lights out. Game over."

"How long before that happens?"

"A month maybe. With luck, a month."

"But you have a play?"

"A new surgical technique. Experimental. If it's successful, you pass Go and get to live a normal life. If it isn't, you either die on the table or suffer a massive stroke."

"Massive?"

"As in, likely to leave you totally incapacitated."

"You believe in predestination?"

"That's not the question."

"Hard to argue with the logic. God is omnipotent and omniscient—all powerful and all knowing. He, or she, or it, knows the day I am to die. If I don't die on that day then God isn't omniscient. That can't be. So the day of my death is already set. It is a date certain. Nothing you, or me, or anyone else can do about it."

"You're not going to draw me into one of your convoluted arguments on the phone."

"I can't assume that you believe in predestination?"

"Or the Tooth Fairy."

"How about reincarnation, then, the Tibetan Buddhist idea of the Wheel of Things—the idea that we keep coming back after each life and are given the chance to lead a worthier one until we finally win our way into Nirvana? You might come back as anything. Monk wanted to come back as a blue teapot, remember?"

"I remember. Not that, either."

"You've a helluva bedside manner."

"I try to give my patients comfort and cheer."

"What would you do?"

"I don't know, Jordy. Punt."

There is still enough light to make out dimples in the river where rainbow are rising.

But the fisherman has left.

Be on the water before first light, stay till the last light goes. That was Uncle Cal's rule.

A month?

It would be early October then. Elkhorn would be prime. Him, too. Never better. All systems go.

Except for this thing Danny's found. Ah, damn.

Jordan looks up to find the first star, discovers it peeping out in the dome of a sky not yet fully dark, recites the little rhyme, makes his wish, finishes his drink, and goes in.

SUNDAY, SEPTEMBER 9
Day Two

Early the next morning, dew sparkling on the empty plains, he is on his way home. Not to the place he lives now. To the place where he started.

He had flown into Denver from San Francisco three days ago, picked up a car and headed north. Up past Medicine Bow and across the great bowl of high prairie to the lodge. No signs of habitation anywhere. Long stretches of empty highway. Lonely country. Starkly beautiful.

Now he's heading east to Casper, angling away from the river, an occasional house setting back a fence-lined lane, big-rigs and farm trucks sharing the road. Should be at the Casper airport by eight. He read somewhere that they trained bomber pilots in World War II there. Grab some coffee. Be on his way.

Two grand days fishing on the North Platte. Rainbows and browns. Taking both wets and dries. Sometimes they hit so hard it felt like a hammer, sometimes soft as a whisper.

He was exhausted at the end of each day. Deliciously. The twilight ritual of drinks on the porch while night rose and the river went still—there was so much comfort and relief all around that he felt the water gods might have cast a spell on him.

Okay.

Catch the morning flight out of Casper to Chicago, make the United connection at O'Hare and be in Louisville by nightfall.

By the time he has his bag and has picked up a car, it's full dark. Commuter traffic on the beltway around town is easing. Most of the gainfully employed are home or almost there.

He'll head east to the interstate. Be there in an hour or so.

He'll catch a late dinner at the little restaurant on the corner across from the Old Capitol. Shouldn't be many people there at that hour. Should be able to get in and out unremarked upon. Then after, cross the railroad tracks and walk the darkened Capitol grounds through the shadows. Memories rising. Looking for Jordy.

Maybe.

Then back to the friendly little bar at the rear of the restaurant. A nightcap. One drink. Or two. Might help some, but won't get him through the night.

He hasn't called Liddy yet. Wasn't up to it last night—and it was too early this morning to wake her. He'll call her tomorrow. Explain where he is and why. She'll be hurt he isn't coming to her.

"Eagle Rare." Jordan says. "Neat."

The bartender nods, pauses, a do-I-know-you look on his face. Doesn't make a connection but sees something that strikes a chord.

"Neat it is."

He turns and reaches to select a bottle from the collection on the shelf behind the bar, says as he turns back, "You look familiar. But I can't place you."

Jordan has been paying no attention, has been focused on a painting on the wall—a stretch of creek with sycamores lining the bank, maybe Elkhorn, not awfully good but good enough to take him back. He looks around, studies the barkeep—an everyday face, starched white shirt, red bowtie, gold wedding band on the hand with which he's pushing the drink forward. Left hand. A left-handed barkeep. What's that saying about lefties? God made everyone right-handed. Only the truly gifted overcome it. Smiles at the thought.

"Saw you crossing the street from the Capitol grounds. Not many people go walking around there this time of night."

The restaurant is almost empty. There is a couple in a booth toward the front. The man has his back to Jordan. Can't make out his face. The woman is searching for something in her purse. They appear indifferent to each other. A party of six is seated by the big window that looks out on the Old Capitol— men in dark suits and muted ties. They don't seem local. Lobbyists probably, or contractors come to paw at the people's coffers. No one else is at the bar.

Jordan smiles back at the barkeep, tells himself be friendly. Charm him, buddy. That's your stock-in-trade. Finish your drink. Wish him a good night. Get out of there.

But the barkeep makes the connection.

"You're the writer. Used to live here. Recognized you from the picture in the paper."

Pleased with himself, the barkeep beams, reaches over to shake his hand.

Jordan takes it. He's surprised at the boost this little bit of recognition gives him. Vanity, thy name is Jordy.

He acknowledges his identity, tries to look modest, pleads an early day tomorrow, and makes his escape.

Eagle Rare does not get him through the night.

He dozes some, dreams some. But doesn't remember the dreams when he wakes and is left with only their residue, which further compounds his attempt at sleep, and so he frets and tosses, wishing fervently for dawn.

He's awake at four. Hears the clock in the Court House tower strike the hour. Realizes sleep won't come, feels it's better to be awake and in command of his thoughts than let them run amok in the semi-consciousness of drowsy sleep.

He gets up, pulls on a pair of jeans and slips a sweat jersey over his head. It is still full dark. He eases quietly out of his room and along the hall so as not to disturb the sleepers. His car is close. Jordan finds it and heads down the hill ... to his yesterdays.

Talking to himself, Jordan slows at the crest of the hill. The valley opens out before him. He can trace the river's path by the mist hanging over it and the outline of the valley by the lighter dark of the sky above the ridgelines.

He pulls on to the overlook, gets out, walks to the railing, stands motionless. The town is down there. Asleep.

Why the hell is he here?

Should he be here at all?

Full daylight soon.

A few lights are blinking on in the valley. The morning breeze is soft. A new day coming, an unsullied day. The first day of whatever is left.

See Uncle Calum. Talk with Billy. Talk with the Colonel. See Aunt Maggie.

Decide.

MONDAY, SEPTEMBER 10
Day Three

It's a little after four in the afternoon. He's showered. Shaved. Clean khakis and a blue button-down wool shirt under the bush jacket.

Walking up St. Clair to Cindy Carlson's office.

No one is expecting him. There is no reason why he should be here. He doesn't want to reveal his condition, doesn't want the concern or the sympathy that admission would bring. He needs some simple explanation that will satisfy his friends and blunt the apprehensions of the few who might be uneasy at his presence.

And Liddy.

He must, without delay, explain to Liddy.

He'll call her tonight. At cocktail time. Her cocktail time. Six-ish on the Coast. Nine-ish for him. Let him get dinner out of the way. Get his case prepared. He will write it out, or at least make notes. Writing it will help him get his thinking clear, decide in advance the best way to say a thing. He'll practice it. He's good at delivering written lines as if they've just come to mind.

It will be a little early for a brandy, but he'll have one anyway.

When he was a young man, when Cindy Vail, now Carlson, was voted most popular girl and the best dancer in the class, St. Clair was a vibrant thoroughfare of shops and stores crowded with people, and the town was the bustling commercial hub of the entire county. Most of the businesses have deserted downtown now for the shopping centers that serve the growing suburbs. He catches his reflection in the plate-glass window of an empty storefront that he is almost certain used to be Farrington's Emporium, the Finest Fashions in the Bluegrass. The girls all got their prom dresses there.

The store is gone. The girls are women now.

She's standing by the receptionist's desk in conversation when he enters. He sees the woman but remembers the girl—the lithe, vivacious, delicious girl.

She still looks delicious. Some of the effect is the way she's dressed, he knows that—an elegantly understated jacket and skirt that highlight her form and her face—and the make-up, he knows that. But there is no way that artifice alone can create the effect Cindy has on the eye and the libido. Every time he sees her there is that involuntary moment of wonder about what might have been.

Cindy looks around to welcome whomever the unannounced visitor might be, steps back in surprise when she sees him, stands a moment in disbelief, then has him a happy embrace, kisses him, and leads him into her office as the receptionist stares.

"Shame on you. You didn't let anyone know you were coming."

She's animated, her hands clasping his as they sit across from each other.

"Everyone will be so pleased. We'll have a party."

He laughs, "Cindy, please."

"No arguments. It's been ages since you were here. How long can you stay?"

Jordan leans back, all hopes of a slipping in unnoticed vanishing in the onslaught of Cindy's enthusiasm.

He should have remembered that Cindy would be Cindy. Make him welcome. Get some friends together. Show him off. He imagines there is a touch of that in the back of her mind. His piece on meth in the mountains won a Pulitzer nomination last year, generated a fair amount of attention, including the story in the Journal the Serafini's barkeep remembered.

He's a celebrity of sorts—minor by any reckoning, but he's a local boy and that counts. Cindy basks in attention. He'd forgotten. In school, she was the homecoming queen. He was the captain of the football team. He was never quite sure which appealed to her more—him or their popularity.

He smiles. Didn't matter. They were having too good a time.

"You're smiling," she says. "We'll do it. Tell me what night."

Laughing now. Impossible not to be caught up in her eagerness.

"I love your parties, but first I need your help."

She releases his hands. Sits back, a questioning frown taking over the smile.

"And I thought you came all this way just to see me. What are you up to, Jordy Jordan?"

In the warmth of Cindy's welcome, Jordan has forgotten momentarily what brought him home. He wonders if this will be the pattern of his time here. Will he become so relaxed in the company of his friends that the sting of it will go away, so comforted in the arms of home that the urgency of it will fade? Will he create a little world of yesterday and slide into it and pull it over his head and make the bad vibes stop?

Cindy, reacting to his silence and the look on his face, "What is it? Are you in trouble?"

"No. Oh, no, nothing like that. I got lost in memories for a moment."

He rises, walks to the window, looks out, then back, and sits down again, leaning forward, smiling, convincingly he hopes, takes her hand.

"When I said I need your help ... "

And now he unfolds his story, the song and dance that will explain why he's come back and keep his secret until he decides to share it—if he decides to share it.

"I'm chasing a story."

"Here? What's interesting enough here to get your attention?"

"Honest Dick Tate."

"Who?"

"The universally admired Treasurer of the grand and glorious Commonwealth of Kentucky who cleaned out the state's coffers one fine spring afternoon, boarded a train to Louisville, and was never heard of again. Biggest robbery in the history of this or any other state. Clean getaway."

"Oh, Jordy. Where did you get such a wild story?"

"Not wild. It's all on the record. Russ Hatter has it all. He put me on to it."

"That's what you're here for?"

"It's a great story. How did he get away with it? What happened to all that money? Russ pointed me to a place where the answers might lie."

Cindy laughs and claps her hands. "Oh, Jordy, this is so exciting. I can help?" She's leaning in eagerly, expectantly.

"I need a place where I can stay and work. A place with privacy. Where I can work undisturbed. Can you find such place for me?"

"How long would you need it?"

"A month. Not sure."

She frowns, thinking. Then nods. "I think I know just the place. Maybe. But what do I say when people ask why you're here?"

"Best not to mention the Honest Dick Tate affair. Could be a sensitive subject with some. Leads might dry up. Doors close. Say, I'm here on a short visit, unwinding from an assignment, going to do some fishing, visit a few friends, relax and think great thoughts. That ought to do."

Jordan has no intention of doing a story on Honest Dick or anyone else. The idea popped into his head as he walked up St. Clair. It would make a good story, even a book. He might even look into it if there was time. There isn't. Now it's just a handy excuse to serve as his cover if Cindy, as is entirely likely, can't resist telling a friend why ole Jordy is really in town.

Later now. Back at the hotel on the hill.

Time for the call to Liddy.

She picks up on the fourth ring, just as the "I'm-not-here-leave-a-message" recording begins to kick on.

"Jordan?"

He met Lydia Bacarro on an evening like this almost three years ago at party for Dan Moran and his soon-to-be bride. Danny was a just year into his new role as head of the department of Neurological Surgery at the University of California San Francisco Medical Center. Dan's now-wife, Gabriella, is Liddy's sister.

Liddy listens without interruption. Which is one of the many things Jordan admires about her. When he finishes, she's silent. He can hear her breathing. Absorbing it. Waiting for it to register. A protective reaction. He knows.

"So, you're going to stay there?"

"For a while.

"Shouldn't you be here talking with Dan about this surgery, learning all you can about it?"

"Yes."

"Why aren't you?"

"Right now I need to be here."

"Why?"

"Sanctuary."

"I don't understand."

"Home ground, Liddy."

Liddy has no idea what this means. There is something in the air, some magic in the night there that can cushion the torment of the decision he has to make? The life-or-death decision, it's there in that little town?

Answers are what he needs.

Answers are what she can help him with.

Come home, Jordan.

But she doesn't say this.

She says, "Home ground," pauses as if examining the idea, is silent for what seems too long, then, at last, says. "All right, love. Goodnight."

On short notice after the call from Jordan, Liddy has invited herself to dinner at her sister's.

They're in the kitchen of the Morans' apartment on Parnassus in walking distance of the Medical Center. Her sister Gabriella sits across from her. Dan Moran is opening the second bottle of chardonnay.

"Why is he there, Dan? Why doesn't he come home?"

"He is home, Liddy."

"No he isn't. He lives here. Here is home."

"This is a place, Liddy, not home. Everywhere he's lived, they're places. Home is where he is now."

Liddy starts to protest. Dan stops her.

"It's the Irish in him. The ancient Celts believed that land that nourishes the mother—the water she drinks, falling from the sky onto the land where she was born and raised; the food she eats that has been grown in the soil of that place; the air she breathes, enriched with the pollen of the grasses and the trees and the flowers of her growing up—all this she absorbs into in her blood. Her blood nourishes the child in her womb, is absorbed into its blood, too. Regardless of where the child wanders or for however long, it is a part of him. It's where his roots are."

Dan refills her glass. Refills Gabriella's. Pours himself a black coffee and sits down.

"There is a hole on a creek there we used to fish when we were boys. It's called Hawk's Hole. A steep cliff overhangs it. On top, there is a ring of boulders that makes a natural fort. Sometimes we'd camp there, pretend at night we were fighting off the monsters attacking the kingdom. We never lost. We felt safe there. Invincible. We were only ten or eleven, but I remember the feeling. He's in his fort. He's looking for that kind of feeling again now."

"Monsters!" Liddy bursts out. "Oh, Dan, not you, too!"

He's startled, but then begins to laugh. Gabriella does as well. Liddy frowns, but her anger fading in their warmth, can't help but join in.

"You Kentucky boys. What did they raise you on—make-believe and moonshine?"

They've moved to the living room. Liddy is on the couch, leaning forward, listening intently. Gabriella, on the couch beside her, sitting back, legs curled beneath her, has her hand on Liddy's shoulder.

Dan is trying to help Liddy grasp the dilemma Jordan faces.

"If he opts for the surgery and it is successful, Jordan can expect to live a normal life span. If it's unsuccessful, he could die on the table. Or worse for him, suffer the effects of a stroke that could cripple him, leave him helpless."

Liddy shudders.

"Tell me again."

"The aneurism is at a spot in the brain where, at the current state of the art, we can't operate. In time, it will rupture. When that happens, his brain will be flooded with blood and he'll die."

"But you have a technique?"

"An extraordinarily delicate procedure. Experimental. Unproven. We think it will produce a successful result, but we won't know until it's tried on a living patient."

"Jordan."

"The alternative is to forgo the procedure. In that case, he's gambling that the aneurism will hold."

"Will it?"

"No."

Dan stops. Liddy closes her eyes, sighs. Gabriella, beside her, reaches and takes her hand. The three sit there in a silence so intense it seems a shout.

TUESDAY, SEPTEMBER 11
Day Four

Jordan is at breakfast at the hotel on the hill, considering.

The Date Certain. That would be a Wednesday. The tenth day of October. No moon that night … the dark of the moon that night. Does this mean something? Is there some omen in this conjunction that he ought to see?

Three days already gone.

Twenty-seven left.

Throughout his career he's worked to deadlines. Never missed one.

What would happen if he missed this one? The thought makes him laugh to himself.

A message is waiting when he returns to his room. "Found the perfect place. Call me. Cindy."

Early afternoon.

Jordan meets her, following the directions she's given him up out of town and east on country roads. Ten miles or so.

When he finds the place, it's a small cottage in a stand of trees on the edge of a meadow. She's sitting in a rocking chair on the porch. As he drives up, he can see that the porch wraps all the way around the house and, to the rear, he catches the glint of sunlight on water.

She rises as he parks, comes down the steps with arms open and a triumphant smile.

"Ta! Da!" she exclaims and sweeps her arm back in an engulfing gesture. "You are going to love it."

The cottage is on a slight rise. There is a wide expanse of meadow behind it that slopes down to the creek. Big oaks give it shade. There is a green canoe pulled up on the grass beside a sycamore. He can hear the whisper of water sliding by.

She takes his hand and pulls him up on the porch.

"Two bedrooms. One will make a den where you can work. There is a nice little kitchen. Indoor plumbing. A great room with a fireplace. And the rocker and canoe. Perfect."

She's bubbling with delight.

"Look around. Hay fields on both sides, corn across the road. The closest neighbor is a quarter of a mile away. The only lights you'll see at night will be your own, the only sounds the sound of the creek and the birds. The phone is unlisted. There is a radio, but not TV. Tell me that's not privacy. Tell me that's not perfect."

Cindy is almost breathless. She's dressed in jeans, a white button-down man's shirt knotted at the waist, her hair tied back and held by a bright red band, looking so girlish and so pleased with herself that he laughs and claps in appreciation.

She's taken aback momentarily, then glows, kisses him on the cheek, and in her excitement, says, "I knew you'd like it. I know what you like."

Then, unsure of how that might be taken, she grabs his hand and whirls him inside to inspect the house.

"It's Judge Fawcett's place." They're in the great room. It has oak paneled walls, a floor-to-ceiling brick fireplace, a picture window with a wide view of the meadow and the creek. Thankfully, no trophy mounts on the walls.

"I thought of it immediately when you mentioned what you wanted. The Judge is on a cruise and won't be back until late October. A small farmhouse was here originally. He tore it down and built this when he bought the land. He uses it as a summer place. I wired him as soon as you left yesterday. It's all yours."

He hadn't expected to be so lucky. The place has the solitude he wants. Some of the finest smallmouth water in the South is practically in his backyard.

Is this a sign? Is his luck changing?

But then reminds himself ... don't grasp at straws, ole buddy.

Cindy is frowning, waiting for his answer. Should she have checked with him first?

"Is that okay?" uncertainty in her voice, concern on her face.

Jordan frowns, pretends to be considering for no reason other than to tease her, then smiles, "It's perfect."

SATURDAY, SEPTEMBER 15
Day Eight

Jordan is settled.

Liddy has searched his closets and shipped him the clothes he's asked her to find, plus a few things she likes and thinks he ought to have on hand. He can feel comfortable in society now.

The cottage on the creek is cleaned and stocked. Cindy has seen to that.

All this activity has allowed him to keep his concentration on practical matters and not be consumed by wrestling with the decision he has to make.

His mood is good. He's glad to be home.

But...

If he lets himself, he can feel doom impending. So he doesn't let himself. It's early September. Just enough autumn in the air for the mornings to be crisp and a bit of color beginning to show in the trees. Elkhorn is running clear and the smallmouth are hungry. He feels fine. No room for doom in this picture. He's of a Scarlett O'Hara frame of mind.

So far, he's seen no one but Cindy, made contact with no one but Cindy. He's holding his secret close. As the due date gets closer, as he homes in on a decision, maybe then he'll want and need the sympathy and concern. But not now.

And there is Cindy's dinner party to get through.

Tonight. At the club. Seven-ish. "A nice little intimate dinner," she says. "A few old friends," she says.

Which old friends? Small town. Most had grown up together. They played together, studied together, sang together.

Dated each other.

Married each other. Some did.

Most stayed. A few left.

He did. And Danny did. And Billy, the Reverend William T. Newall. But Billy came back.

Those who stayed are the backbone of the city now. Shelby Crittenden is the proprietor of the county's Ford dealership, TJ Browning a high official in state government, Tom Andrews is the vice-mayor and president of Commonwealth Insurance Company, one of the state's largest.

Who did Cindy choose?

Tom? They were best buddies in high school, teammates on the team that won the conference championship. Danny and Shelby were part of that gang, too, but Danny's in San Francisco. TJ's here, though.

Cindy. Cindy.

The country club is on the east side of town, the Lexington side, where Bluegrass pastures flow to the horizon and princely thoroughbreds grace the landscape. There is no country anywhere more peaceful or more majestic.

The club is up a long, arrow-straight macadam lane, through an entry gate flanked by red brick pillars, to a circular drive, in front of a white columned mansion with rocking chairs on the portico.

The country club is the playground of the monied—the people who run the town, the privileged and the powerful.

So he will be among the privileged and the powerful of the Capital City this night. These will be people he grew up with or knows casually, or who know of him. Jordan knows the wives, or should. They are all local girls. Except Shelby's wife. From Danville, he thinks. On a Friday night in the main dining room of the club with music for dancing, likely a quorum of the city's movers and shakers will be there. Hallelujah, amen.

Cindy has finessed the seating problem. She's gone with a circular table.

It's on the veranda, open to the night, looking out to the course. Jordan is seated facing in, with the 18th green at his back and the fairway stretching out beyond. Twilight is just beginning, and tree-frogs are warming up. The combo in the main dining room is working on a nice, slow tune. Several couples are up dancing. There is a tinkle of laughter and the low hum of happy conversation. A soft autumn night in the midst of Bluegrass gentry.

Except he's not quite sure that Cindy doesn't have some mischief in mind for her own amusement. She has been known to.

Cindy has seated herself to his right; TJ's wife, Mrs. Thomas Jonathan Browning, is to his left. The last time Jordan saw her she was Sue Watson. That was the night before he left for New York. A lifetime ago. They were … he's not sure how he wants to remember it.

They were in college, just on the edge of life. Those memories are locked in one of the little rooms in his mind where he keeps the things he doesn't want to think about. They escape into his dreams sometimes.

He did not make the wedding.

TJ wanted him to be best man. His excuse was distance. He was in Cairo working on a story he could not leave. But of course he could have, had he been brave enough. He has seen TJ on his few trips back, but not Sue. Not Mrs. Thomas Jonathan Browning.

TJ is named for General Thomas Jonathan Jackson— Stonewall Jackson, hero of the Confederacy. He aches to be called Stonewall. It's the perfect nickname for the image he wants for himself. But his father calls him TJ and he's stuck with it and likes it better than Tommy or Johnny or any of the other names they could have hung on him. Sounds mature, serious, a name not to be trifled with.

TJ and Jordan Aimes became fast friends the day they met, smashing into each other in a tackling drill the first day of football practice the fall of their freshman year.

TJ was bigger. Jordan was faster. In the drill, the ball carrier tries to run over, or around, the tackler. Jordan had the ball, came barreling in, took a jig step left to draw TJ off balance, shifted back right, dropped his shoulder and ran with legs pumping hard intending to blow TJ away. TJ didn't take the fake. Hit him head on. Stopped him cold. They struggled against each other. Jordan wouldn't go down. TJ wouldn't budge. Slowly they raised up, straining, not giving an inch, until they were fully upright in the middle of the field, standing motionless, glaring nose to nose.

Someone on the sidelines laughed, and then everyone laughed, and coach came over and took the ball and said, "Stubborn. We can put that to use," slapped TJ on the butt and walked away grinning.

Then they laughed, too. And limped to the sidelines pleased to be in each other's company, and it stayed that way all through school, all through college, and the feeling didn't diminish even when they became men.

Cindy is a keep-the-conversation-lively, boy-girl-boy sort of seater, so the wives are interspersed around the table between men not their husbands—with the exception of Sue, who sits between TJ and Jordan.

The conversation is lively. They're getting caught up on Jordan's wanderings, bringing him up to date on theirs, telling stories of times remembered, laughing at old missteps—the sort of interplay to be expected from old friends getting together with a favored friend after an absence, interrupted occasionally by someone from the main dining room coming out to greet Jordan and welcome him home.

They finish dinner, have their dessert, and are sitting back now over coffee and liquors.

TJ has switched to bourbon neat. His first three were bourbon and branch.

Jordan doesn't remember TJ as a heavy drinker. Hardly a drinker at all. TJ is the one that got them all home after big party nights in college.

Jordan looks questioningly across the table to Tom. Tom frowns, nods his head as if saying "yeah," and mouths the word "later."

TJ rises from his seat. He's a little unsteady but not slurring his words. Taps on his glass with his fork three times. Gets everyone's attention.

"A toast!" TJ turns to Jordan, holds out his glass. "To my good friend. He left us to become famous but comes back to us now and again. For which pleasure we are grateful."

He raises his glass high, "To Jordy Aimes. The best of the best," and drinks it down.

Jordan is both pleased and embarrassed.

While Jordan sorts it out and before he can respond, TJ continues.

"Now, a favor." He sweeps his glass around, taking in the whole table.

"You all know what a clumsy dancer I am. But … " he focuses on Sue, "I know how good you are, and … " he points his glass at Jordan, "and how good Jordy is … and I remember how great the two of you looked dancing together the night of our senior ball."

He pauses, takes a sip, looks around the table conspiratorially, grinning.

He takes Sue's hand and raises her slowly until she's standing beside him. He motions toward Jordan, turns Sue toward him.

"For old time's sake. Take us all back to that night. I've already arranged it with the band."

Sue turns sharply to TJ, a look of surprise and disbelief, a have-you-lost-your-mind frown forming. Jordan is as taken off guard as Sue.

TJ stands there waiting expectantly, half-plastered and looking pleased with himself. Cindy is smiling. Jordan hesitates for just a moment. Aware the attention of the whole table is on them. Not a time to hesitate. He rises. Moves to Sue's side. Reaches for her hand, hoping his smile and his manner will reassure her.

"Game?"

She doesn't understand at first.

Then does.

And laughs. And takes his hand.

"You've always had such a way with words."

She was pretty and smart and liked even by some of the girls who envied her.

Her father was one of most powerful men in town, president of the biggest bank and a man of unshakeable and uncompromising commitment to the teachings and requirements of his Holy Catholic Church. As a consequence, Sue was allowed to date only those boys from what he considered to be good families and whose conduct was exemplary. Good Catholic boys were preferred, though not all of them made the cut. TJ was the only one of Jordan's crowd that did, and he just barely.

Jordan took Sue's off-limits status as a challenge. He flirted with her outrageously. To his surprise, she flirted back.

They teased, and laughed, and studied together and over the course of the year (their senior year; they had paid no attention to each other earlier), they became very good friends. As sometimes happens, that friendship began to segue into something more intimate.

But TJ was the boy she was permitted to date, and Cindy was Jordan's girl. Out of the strictures of high-school propriety, they tried to ignore the feeling that something was urging them to be more than friends.

Graduation came.

The big night. The big dance. At the Club House on the cliff above the river overlooking the dam.

Jordan took Cindy. TJ was with Sue.

The boys in tuxes, the girls in gowns.

Corsages and boutonnieres.

Moonlight and music.

A few half-pints in the jackets of the worldlier. Flavor the Coke with a little bourbon, a touch of gin for the Seven-Up.

They were all at the same table—Jordan and Cindy, TJ and Sue, Tom and Danny and Shelby and their dates. They were light-hearted and happy.

Tom had the flask.

Late in the evening, toward the end, Cindy is dancing with Tom. She's the best dancer in the class. Guys keep cutting in. Jordan's at the table, watching appreciatively. TJ sits across with Sue beside him. Sue is almost as popular as Cindy, but with the embargo on who she is allowed to date, she's been spending most of the evening enduring TJ's shuffling, and they are sitting out this dance when TJ, for reasons known only to himself, but possibly out appreciation of Sue putting up with his awkward attempts, leans across the table to Jordan.

"Do me a favor. Dance with this girl. She's worn me out."

Sue looks up, surprised, then impishly, at Jordan.

Jordan is equally as surprised but couldn't be more pleased.

"As a favor," he says, and rises and walks around the table to stand before Sue. He bows, offers his hand and asks laughingly, "Game?"

She smiles coquettishly, lifts her hand to his. "Charmed," she replies and rises.

Doris Day was singing "Secret Love." It was the big song that year. They danced. When the music ended, they were on the patio. It was darker there, shadowed and secluded. Standing face to face, holding hands, looking into each other's eyes, unplanned, unthinking, in the shadows, as natural as breathing, they kissed. This was their only kiss, their only intimacy—until later.

So, the summer ended and they went away to college with that moment in the shadows just a memory ... a memory warming Jordan as he takes Sue in his arms and begins the dance, and Sue, as she rests her cheek against his.

SUNDAY, SEPTEMBER 16
Day Nine

We're back where we began now.

Jordan has made it back to the cottage from Cindy's party, safely through the salubrious night and past the Grim Reaper, risen, shaved, showered, breakfasted, checked the creek for color and is now on Tom Andrews' back patio off the seventh green at the club. Tom and he have finished their round of golf. Twilight is just descending. The scent of roses and fresh mown grass is in the air. Peace all around. Nothing anywhere in sight that might discomfort him. He wonders why he ever left.

In a while, Anna will join them with nibbles of some kind. When it gets darker, Tom will fire up the grill and put the steaks on and they'll sit in the twilight and laugh and talk and enjoy the evening.

"She's still a lovely woman, isn't she? You make a handsome couple."

The dance with Sue—how fast the years fell away for Jordan, how completely they fell away. How different it would have been had he stayed. How different would it have been—if he had stayed?

"Are they doing okay, Sue and TJ?"

"TJ's drinking too much. You saw that last night."

"He was never much of a drinker. What happened?"

Tom hesitates.

They had fashioned themselves the 2nd Street Irregulars. They'd been together since second grade at Second Street school—Jordan, Tom Andrews, Shelby Henderson, and Danny Moran. TJ joined them later, a transfer from a county school.

Jordan was the leader, Tom the Captain of Deviltry. Shelby had the car, Danny the brains. TJ was their minder, the straightest of arrows, guarding their backs and doing his best to keep them out of trouble.

The originals were equals in each other's eyes, competitors at some things. It was different with TJ. He didn't see himself as an equal with Jordan. He wanted to be like Jordan, be as smart and as talented and as popular. Jordan was his hero.

Jordan pretended he wasn't aware of this. But he was, and because of it, he felt a responsibility for TJ that the others didn't. They all felt a certain responsibility for TJ. He was so good natured, so trusting, so guileless that all felt he needed looking out for, but Jordan's was more personal.

Knowing this, Tom is reluctant to surface a problem that Jordan might feel compelled to shoulder.

"The sky is going to fall on him soon. He knows it."

"What kind of trouble is he in?"

"More than he can handle. You'll read about it soon enough in the press."

"Nothing we can do?"

"Nothing."

"It's that bad?"

"A Grand Jury investigation bad enough for you? There is one underway now. It involves the awarding of a contract covering life and medical insurance for state employees. A very big contract. A very lucrative contract. Everyone expected a firm that has been doing business with the state for years to win it. It didn't. Instead, the contract went to a newly formed company that didn't meet the qualifications for bidding and has no track record in insurance of any type. But that company does have some very well-connected names on its board. The losing company cried foul immediately."

"So?"

"TJ is the state official who approved the bid and awarded the contract. The Grand Jury will make its report on Monday. TJ will be indicted and charged with criminal fraud."

"You're serious? TJ? That can't be right. Grand Jury investigations are secret until their indictments are returned. How do you know this?"

"TJ told me. He was undone, scared, needed a friend to lean on, looking for a miracle, knowing there is none. He needed some comfort, the kind the bottle can't give."

"That makes no sense. TJ's not a conniver. He's a Boy Scout—trustworthy, honest, loyal, brave. He'd never have the balls to try to defraud the state, would never even think of trying something like that. This doesn't make any sense."

"It may not to you and me, but the signature on the document is his. There will be a trial. All the dirty details will come out. There are others involved, men who actually devised the scheme and lured TJ into it, but the signature on the document is that of Thomas Jonathan Browning, Deputy Commissioner, Department of Finance, the official with the authority to award the contract. His signature. No one else's."

"Criminal fraud? How bad is that?"

"Conviction carries a ten-year minimum sentence. A plea deal might lessen that, but in any event, prison."

"Does Sue know?"

"She has to suspect something because of TJ's drinking, but he hasn't told her. His pride wouldn't let him. The shame will devastate his family. His mother, Sue, they won't be able to hold their heads up. His father, you know how prideful he is. The press will go on for weeks."

"There is nothing we can do—attorneys, pleas for clemency, nothing?"

"Later, maybe. After the trial, work with the DA, try to influence the sentencing recommendation, work on getting him assigned to a livable prison. After the furor dies down, work on getting a pardon. Now, nothing. You wouldn't have time, anyway," Tom says, half joking, trying to lighten the mood. "You'll be too busy unraveling the mystery of Honest Dick Tate and all that missing money."

Jordan's mind is still on TJ's plight. The change of subject distracts him, brings him back to now, back to Tom's patio, with a pleasant day winding down.

"Cindy! I should have known better."

"You did know better. You knew she wouldn't keep it to herself. I think that's what you had in mind all along."

"How many people do you think she's told?'

"Anyone who's interested. The half of the town that's not interested will be told anyway."

They shake their heads laughing and are reaching for another beer as Anna walks out.

"What are you two finding so funny?"

"We're talking about why Jordan decided to come visit."

"It's a secret," she says, crinkling her nose at Jordan, "but I understand that he's come to work on a story about a man who walked off with the whole state treasury and was never heard of again."

She bends over and kisses Jordan on the cheek, "We don't care what the reason is. We're just happy to see him. Now buy me a drink and light the grill."

When they've finished dinner, it's gotten cooler. Anna goes inside to watch the late news while Tom and Jordan have their nightcap. They're sitting around the fire pit on the pond side of the patio, talking and watching little embers float up in the dark and die, letting a nice mellow port soothe out the evening.

And the question comes, the one he doesn't want.

"So, what's the real reason?"

Ah, damn. Do a little song and dance, try a bit of fancy footwork. Keep it light. Tom won't press it. He leans forward, pats Tom on the knee.

"I just couldn't stay away any longer. I had to come back for the pure pleasure of your company, old friend, for the pure pleasure of your company."

Tom shakes his head knowingly as they both laugh and let it go.

When he leaves, Jordan turns back to Tom, "Nothing to be done about TJ? You're sure?"

"Nothing," Tom says. "Leave it alone. You'll read about it soon enough."

Later, back at the cottage, Jordan gets a fire going to add a little cheer, then finds the phone and places the call to Liddy.

"Come home." Her voice is soft, comforting.

Saturday night in San Francisco. It's a fine night there—he checked—a crisp, clear night with stars sparkling and little fingers of fog beginning to reach in over the bay. If he were there, they would be finishing up dinner over a bottle of a good pinot, or already at the bar at the Comstock with friends and talk.

"It's been a week since you called."

"I got distracted."

He tells her about TJ, and that he misses her and wishes she was here to keep him warm. It's raining, and it's cold and grim outside, and he needs her to make the phantoms go away.

And she says, teasingly, "I can do that."

Then not teasing, "I can be on a plane tomorrow ... if you want."

The want of her was a feeling tugging at him as he talked. The saying of it soothed him. But he had no thought of asking her to come. He isn't far enough along. He isn't far along at all. There was the getting in and getting settled to attend to, the reconnoitering and the remembering. And now, this situation with TJ. Things to do, people to see. So much to occupy his mind. So much to let him slip into and hide behind.

She'll have in her mind the decision she wants him to make. She won't push it. Won't even say it. But it will be in her mind and she won't be able to mask it.

She wants honesty from him in all things. Insists so. He believes she believes it, but he also knows that honesty is a dangerous commodity. He is very careful with the truth he tells.

He can't make his decision with her holding his hand. So he tells her, "Later is when I'll need you most."

Which is the God's honest truth.

Her response is slow in coming. She's turning this over in her mind, wondering. When her response does come, it catches him completely off guard.

"Will you take me to Hawk's Hole?"

"How do you know Hawk's Hole?"

"Dan told me. I want to see the monsters."

"The monsters?" He's taken aback, then remembering and laughing says, "Not to be missed."

They chat happily for a while then, both warming to the banter and the comfort of each other's voice. She misses him. He misses her. That is enough to convey, after they've hung up, the apprehension of what it would be like if the missing turns out to be permanent. It will gnaw at them both.

They go on for a while, Jordan keeping the flow going, reluctant to surrender to the loneliness of the night.

She catches his mood in his tone.

"Are you ….?"

She stops, hesitates, doesn't continue, lets the unasked question hang.

But he knows.

And fills the silence with a soft "No."

"No. I'm not," he repeats, and knows that she knows he's answering her unasked question.

"Getting late," he says. "Better let you go. Early day tomorrow."

She's embarrassed at her intrusion into a matter so private to him, as bad as asking do you love me, which she has not done. But she can think of nothing else to say, only, "Let me know when you want me to come. Don't wait so long to call again. Sweet dreams."

No, he's not afraid.

Not yet.

Jordan is an only child.

His dad died young. On a trip to the headwaters of the Rockcastle River after walleye. Peritonitis killed him before they could get him down out of the mountains and to a doctor.

He was in his early thirties.

His mother was twenty-nine. She was the loveliest, sweetest young woman in the whole damn county.

She was one of seven—four boys, three girls. Her family coalesced around them and Jordan grew up in the midst of a clan of hardworking, good-natured uncles; loving, bossy aunts; and more cousins than he could count.

He attended the local grade and high school, was good at sports, president of the debate club, editor of the school newspaper. He chose Kentucky for his college, just up the road at Lexington. He was no scholar, but he was bright and curious and interested in almost everything—except numbers and test tubes. His inclinations ran to words and ideas. He thought he might try law school, but became interested in journalism, which road took him to exciting places and put him in the company of interesting people—but has brought him back here now, full circle.

Kentucky is one state in from the Atlantic, through Virginia.

Its Northern border is the Ohio River. On the other side of the river are the states of Ohio, Indiana, and Illinois.

The Southern border is Tennessee.

West Virginia is the Eastern.

The Mississippi River and Missouri form the western.

Jesse Stuart, poet, author, and native son said of it, "If these United States can be called a body, then Kentucky can be called its heart."

The state is divided into five geographic regions. Moving east to west, they are The Eastern Mountains (Appalachia), The Bluegrass (the beautiful land), The Pennyroyal (the west central section of the state—fertile valleys, sparkling streams, and an abundance of caves, including Mammoth Cave), The Western Coal Fields (the richest coal mining region, plus timber and crops), and the Jackson Purchase (the far southwestern tip of the state, the most rural, with great hunting and fishing).

The families Daniel Boone led through The Cumberland Gap to open up the frontier, when they came to The Bluegrass, they thought they had found Eden.

This town he's in is the capital city.

Most people think that Louisville, where they run the Derby and store all that gold at Fort Knox, or Lexington, home of the University of Kentucky and its famous basketball teams, is the capital.

Both cities wanted to be and fought hard to be chosen but lost out to the wily negotiators in the little river town who outmaneuvered them when the decision was being made.

The river had a lot to do with it. The Kentucky River drains the eastern and central parts of the state, running on a diagonal from the Appalachian Mountains in the south to the Ohio River valley in the north. The Ohio, in turn, flows west into the Mississippi, which runs south to New Orleans, opening the way for the timber and minerals of the eastern mountains and the riches of the fertile Bluegrass to get to the waiting markets in New Orleans and the Gulf of Mexico.

In those early days, the 1700s, with few roads, and those which did exist mostly mud and frustration in the winter rains, or dust and pests in the heat of summer—and dangerous and daunting in any season—the river was the fastest, easiest, safest road to the outside world.

Frankfort was the only town of any note along its length, snuggling in the folds of a big, looping S-curve about halfway down.

At the time Jordan was growing up, Frankfort was the second smallest capital city in the country. It still is. Its size is part of its charm. Its setting, in that pastoral valley in the heart of the Bluegrass, with the river winding through it, accounts for the rest.

Both the size of the town, and its setting, are important to understanding Jordan. It was small enough that a boy could know it, explore its streets, plumb its alleys, draw it around him like a comforting blanket—and feel secure. He was safe there, knew there were people around, adults who knew his mom and dad and who knew him and would look out for him if he was lost, or hurt, and see he got safely home, blood kin he could count on, and friends. He had friends all over town.

Home.

It is home.

MONDAY, SEPTEMBER 17
Day Ten

The fields are warming in the morning sun, look fresh and clean.

Jordan is up, making breakfast, wondering if there was enough rain upstream last night to muddy the water and make fishing today a non-starter. He hasn't unlimbered a rod since he's been here. He can hear the creek sliding by outside, pictures himself working a nymph in a seam just below a big rock where the world's record smallmouth is holding.

Last night.

He remembers Tom's remarks about TJ on the brink of a calamity.

And Liddy's concern for his state of mind. Pushes both away. He has pancakes in the skillet and maple syrup warming.

When he was a boy, on weekend mornings when the creek was running clear and the sun not yet up, Uncle Calum would come get him. They'd push across the meadow, slip through the gate at the barbed wire fence, and be on the water before first light—be there when the smallmouth woke.

Those who are not fishermen will not understand what Jordan is remembering or the feeling it sparks.

You need to have held a fly-rod in hand to know about this, to have waded the water, felt the mantle of the morning drape you, made the cast, watched the line roll out in a graceful arc over sparkling riffles, felt the excitement of the strike, played the fish.

This is powerful stuff for those of a certain temperament— those who are partial to solitary endeavors, who take comfort in nature.

This activity is special to Jordan. He can disappear into it. He can turn the world off and lose himself in it. But not today.

Jordan has got to get focused.

If he opts for the procedure, Danny says it must be done as soon as possible. When he makes the decision, he wants to be to be able to do it feeling that he has played the hand he's been dealt as well as circumstance permitted.

Another concern perplexes him.

That line about "the sleep of death." It keeps running through his mind: "In that sleep of death what dreams may come?" Ah, there's the rub. When he steps through that door, what will be there?

An unending nightmare of demons and damnation.

The gate to Eden standing open.

Or nothing.

Nothing. Just nothing at all.

He wonders. Put that question to Billy.

Today is for the Colonel.

Two men have been Jordan's guides.

Mentors is a better word, but it lacks the closeness these men had with Jordan and implies a conferring of favors when all they gave him was their time and concern.

They helped him through his adolescence and early manhood, taught him things he ought to know, showed him pitfalls to avoid. They helped him understand what he was feeling and how to act—things a father would have helped with, but since Jordan lost his father at such a young age, he was without this advantage. More than that, they made sure he knew some of the things a father might think it best to let the boy discover for himself, or not discover at all.

The men were his mother's youngest brother—his Uncle Calum—and Colonel Rook Sinclair, his father's business partner and best friend.

The Colonel lives in a house made of fieldstone on a cliff overlooking the river south of town. A flight of stairs leads down to the water's edge where there is a small dock. He keeps his houseboat tethered there and a johnboat for fishing. Jordan learned to swim from that dock.

"Jordan! Damn it's good to see you, boy. You've been away too long," says the Colonel when Jordan arrives, grabbing him in a bear hug.

"You should have let me know you were coming. Dove season is on. We can set up a hunt." He is beaming, welcoming with undisguised affection.

"Well, here you are. What keeps you looking so young, boy? Clean living? No. It has to be all the excitement in that life you're living. The people, the places. I envy you all that. No, I don't. I'm delighted for you."

He's been saying all this while ushering Jordan to the patio where a table is waiting.

"Sit down, sit down. Let tell me Mae you're here. Make us some coffee. You have to stay for lunch. She's making Hot Browns. Now tell me why you're here. I know it's not this Honest Dick Tate foolishness."

There is just the hint of chill in the air. Fluffy white clouds laze in a clear blue sky. The glint of the river is visible, winding its way through some of the richest farmland in the state, the wooded hillsides turning color. Damn, it's good to be home, Jordan thinks, those were good times, lots of laughter, lots of fun. Not all of it, though. No one makes it through adolescence unbloodied. But the Colonel helped keep Jordan's wounds to a minimum and dodge major disasters. Which is the principal reason Jordan is here. The Colonel's thoughts are what Jordan needs now.

The Colonel's title is an honorific. It is bestowed by the Governor of Kentucky on those who have done remarkable deeds or given outstanding service to the state or nation. It is one of the highest honors the Commonwealth confers. Jordan isn't exactly certain of the reason for Rook Sinclair's commission. The Battle of Hill 937 probably, Hamburger Hill it was called. Ten deadly days of bloody hell in Viet Nam. The 101st Airborne took it and held it…until they were ordered to walk away. After all that blood and all that pain, after all that sacrifice, the high command decided that Hill 937 was not of strategic value after all. Abandon it.

Lieutenant Rook Sinclair's platoon led the attack that took that hill. It earned him a Silver Star.

Jordan often thought about that, about what trick of mind it took to cause a man to run through a cloud of small-arms fire or slash a knife across another man's throat—a courage he wondered if he has, a coldness he thinks he might.

It could have been for that.

Or for something other. The firm the Colonel and Jordan's father established has been remarkably successful. He is a generous supporter of charities and libraries. Good works do sometimes have their reward.

"Are you going to tell me or am I going to have to beat it out of you?"

The Colonel is finishing his coffee and moving the pie plate aside. He's smiling that crinkly, quizzical smile.

Despite the years, he hasn't changed much. Not quite handsome. Close to it, though. Even when he was younger, he didn't have the look of a man who jumped out of airplanes or led desperate attacks up coverless hills. A gymnast's build, not a linebacker's. Definitely not the look of a warrior. Don't count on looks to give the measure of a man.

Jordan laughs, throws up his hands in mock defense.

"I need help with a decision," Jordan says.

"Advice comes with consequences. You might be tempted to take it."

"I've taken it before," Jordan says, no banter in his voice when he says this.

"What kind of decision?"

"One I wish I didn't have to make."

The words hang there, charging the air.

"Of consequence?"

Jordan only nods and to the Colonel's bewilderment, the mood of the day has changed to something very somber. Mae comes to clear the plates away. Neither he nor Jordan says anything as she works. Mae senses their mood.

"You two arguing? You stop that now, Rook Sinclair! Jordan! You be nice," and gives them both a motherly smile and walks away, which softens the edge a bit.

The Colonel pushes back his chair, stands.

"Let's walk," he says, "down to the dock." They often went there when Jordan was a boy, watched the river roll by, talked the problem through, and worked it out.

They take chairs from the deck of the houseboat and place them out on the end of the dock where the sun is warmest. The river here is wide. Ledges of limestone cut by the river as it formed the valley eons ago line the opposite bank. Oaks and sweet gum are on the ridge line and dogwood and laurel on the valley wall. The water is running clear and the current middling.

"How long has it been since we've been together"?

"Three years, about," says Jordan, "when I was working the meth story."

"How old are you now?"

"Forty-eight next month."

"You look as fit as the boy we sent to the big city. You were, what, twenty-one?"

"Twenty-two. I had just gotten my degree. Ready to conquer the world."

"Yes, I remember. You'd had your talk, made your decision, and were eager to get gone. The girl? What was her name?"

Jordan tenses. Frowns. Replies, gaze still out over the water, not looking to the Colonel, "Sue." Stops, then repeats, softly, "Sue. Sue Watson."

The Colonel remembers, too. Remembers the hurt of it. "Sue. Yes. Pretty girl. Thoughtful girl. I liked her. Banker Watson's daughter."

Jordan had come to him with it. They had talked it through here, looking out over the river like this. The Colonel had told Jordan what he knew to be true—that life is a series of trade-offs. To get something of value, you have to give something of value. The exchange is never equal. That makes no difference so long as what you're getting is worth, to you, what you're willing to give. Make sure you understand what the price is, though. Had he?

"She married your friend TJ. Yes, well. And off you went and now here you are with the world your oyster and another consequential decision to make. What could that concern? You're not married. No children. You're an only child, so no siblings. Your mother, bless her heart, isn't with us any longer. No close family to worry about.

"Your talents are in demand. No money problems. No one's suing you for character assassination. The meth mob? They're all still in jail, so there shouldn't be any noteworthy threat from that department.

"Women? You haven't gotten someone pregnant?"

"Lord, no!" Jordan says, waving away the thought.

"I give up then. What's brought you here with so heavy a load?"

The afternoon is almost gone by the time they finish.

They had sat looking out across the river, not at each other but side by side, as Jordan talked. Not being thrown off by the emotions playing on another's face, not hindered by concerns of whether his own fears and weaknesses were on display, talking as if he were talking to himself, talking to the water, talking to the wind, Jordan could be as honest as if he was, as open as he can be, not knowing fully what he feels or fears.

And the Colonel listens, with no interruptions, no words of sympathy or solace, just singular attention. When Jordan stops, the only fitting comment is silence—Jordan emptied by what he has said, the Colonel absorbing the weight of it. How long they sat in that silence neither remembers.

"It is an awful gamble you have to take," the Colonel says at last. He stands then and, looking down on Jordan still seated, says, "This decision you have to make, before you make it you need to know something you don't know yet. That's why you're here. You're trying to retrieve something that you lost or left here, or learn something you forgot or never knew. I don't know what that is. If I can help find it, you know I will."

He turns then, looks away from Jordan and out over the river.

"Light's going. We should be heading up."

Mae is watching from the kitchen window as they come up the hill. She notes the Colonel's hand on Jordan's shoulder, sees the handshake at the car, watches as the Colonel stands watching Jordan out of sight, then walks slowly, head down, back to the house.

Mae has been Rook Sinclair's cook and housekeeper since her sister Tracey died. She knows Rook's affection for the boy and his for Rook. Their mood at lunch troubled her. That feeling is gone, but a good one hasn't replaced it. Whatever they were discussing has saddened him.

TUESDAY, SEPTEMBER 18
Day Eleven

For the first time since this began, Jordan has slept the whole night through.

The talk with the Colonel yesterday, it freed him. Jordan had been holding his circumstance tight into himself, had told no one but Liddy, had examined it with no one. Not even Liddy. Except the Colonel now. And in doing that, has for the first time truly begun to examine it himself. Actually face it. Actually accept the fact of it. That was strangely liberating.

He slept.

Unmolested. And woke emboldened.

Twenty days to Date Certain.

Damn if he was going to spend all of those cogitating on the cataclysmic.

It's too late to be on the water before first light, but there is bound to be a decent hatch just before nightfall. Time for Cal Macklin.

The hatch came off as is should have. Late afternoon. Slightly overcast. Midges. Hordes of them, microscopically small little black dots dimpling the water and smallmouth rising to take them.

Wading thigh deep in gently flowing water, they threw phantoms and bead-heads and had limited out in less than an hour. Nothing of brag-able size, but a smallmouth of any size is a worthy fight. They had entered the creek at their favorite spot at the foot of the meadow off the road to Peaks Mill and are now on the road back to Calum's.

"It's a beautiful stretch of creek."

Jordan nods and smiles. The pool runs almost eighty yards along the edge of the meadow. Sycamores are scattered on both sides. A wide riffle sits at its head, slowing the current and feeding the creek into a long run flowing just fast enough to keep a fly moving enticingly, but not so strong as to make wading difficult. The run of the stretch is open to the sky and there is ample room for backcasts, so long casts can be made and their elegance admired. The banks are mostly stones and pebbles. Bushes overhang. The stream bed is gravel. A few small, slightly submerged boulders break the surface intermittently. It is one of the most peaceful places Jordan knows.

"They say you can't step into the same river twice. I can. Every time I step into Elkhorn I'm home."

"Why?"

"Pardon?"

"Why are you here? It's been years since I've seen you and all at once you appear out of the blue wanting to go fishing. What's triggered you?"

"You don't know about the Honest Dick Tate story?"

"The only person who believes that is Cindy Carson," Cal says laughing.

They're driving. They are on a narrow country back-road. The light is fading. There is a pull-out ahead, one of the pull-outs the county places along the creek to accommodate fishermen and kayakers. Jordan brakes suddenly and pulls in. Cal jerks forward, looks around baffled, "What happened, what's wrong?"

Jordan eases the car to a stop, punches off the ignition, turns slowly to his uncle, motions to the door, opens his and steps out, waits for Cal to follow.

Cal has no idea what's going on, Jordan no plan in mind. At the side of the pull-out nearest the creek there is one of those long trestle type wooden tables with a bench down either side. Jordan motions to Cal to sit, stays standing himself.

"You still carry that flask."

Cal is trying to puzzle out what's going on. He has that what-the-hell-is-happening look, but nods yes, and unbuttons the flap on his fishing vest. Out comes a flask, silver, slightly dented, a treasured veteran of dove hunts and tailwater streams, of tailgate parties and hard-won wins.

"Eagle Rare?"

"Blanton's."

"The first sip I ever had was out of that flask. What was it?"

"Your first dove hunt? With the Colonel? Harper's, probably."

"Let me see if this is better."

"Nothing is better than the first taste." He passes the flask. "Now, dammit, what's going on!"

Jordan has himself together now. This will do fine. Better than back at Cal's, out here in the privacy of the open, just trees and night birds, and the creek whispering over stones.

"Remember the time I came to you after my talk with Sue Watson's father?"

Cal fixes Jordan with a frowning stare, then reaches for the flask, takes his swallow without his eyes leaving Jordan's face.

Jordan stares just as intently back. "Remember what you told me?"

It was a spring day that day, late May, summer waiting to start. When he arrived, he was as angry as Cal had ever seen him ... and as indignant.

Jordan was a week away from donning his cap and grown, getting his diploma, and heading out into the eagerly waiting world. They were making plans for a big going-away party, the handshakes and kisses of congratulations, the start of a career they all were certain would be exciting and successful.

"Yes, I remember," Cal says slowly, softly. "So ...." And waits.

Jordan was nine when his father died. Calum was twenty. They were in each other's life until Jordan went away to college. Those were the years in which Jordan was coming of age, was learning what proud men do and how they conduct themselves, what honor means and why it must be maintained, why manners are important and boasting shameful. And girls, of course, he was learning about girls ... about what pleasures they are, and what dangers accompany them. Cal gave Jordan a small notebook (three-ring, burgundy leather cover) to write all those rules down in—canons to be studied and thought on.

The Macklins were among the county's earliest settlers and most prominent farmers. It was assumed that Calum would be, too. All his brothers were. But Calum's talent was music, not planting and harvesting. He was gifted with the guitar and banjo, could get all the joy and melancholy that was in a mandolin out of it, and had a fine baritone singing voice.

Calum was the baby of the family and was doted on and indulged and when the time came to grow up and he told them that music was his calling, not a one of them objected. We have enough farmers, his brothers agreed. Go make us proud, they said.

So he formed a little Bluegrass band, called it Cal Macklin and the Good Ole Boys and was soon the toast of half the state. The ladies loved him. The men cheered his riffs. He was a happy young man living life as a game, and he the winner.

The thing that most appealed to Jordan about his uncle Cal was that he was like sunshine in the gloom. He was bold and strong and brimming with cheer. He seemed to enjoy every moment, savor every experience. That was one of the reasons his music was so liked. It moved the listener onto that plane with him.

A better mentor for Jordan during those years would have been impossible to find.

They are in Cal's office in the little studio in the meadow behind the main house at the farm. Jordan is standing in the doorway in jacket and tie, neatly creased chinos, shoes shined—fuming.

"I got a summons today."

"Close the door, you're letting the flies in," Cal says. "Summons? Like a command to appear?"

"Like a command to appear. From Mr. Watson."

Andrew Watson was, even at rest, imperial. Every community, large or small, has its aristocracy. As the chairman of the city's largest bank, Andrew Watson sat at the pinnacle of this one's.

The message was delivered by his secretary. She was friendly enough, "Mr. Watson would like to see you. Today. At three-thirty. In his office. Thank you."

There was no "if you please," or "if that is convenient," or "if you can make it."

If Mr. Watson wished to see you, you came.

Jordan skipped his afternoon class, hurried to his apartment, changed, and made the drive from the campus to be in Watson's office in the bank in Frankfort by two-forty-five. Punctuality is next to godliness. He had met Watson only once and that just in passing. Jordan doesn't know what this is about. He thinks he can guess.

After the single kiss in the shadows on the patio that high school graduation night, Jordan and Sue Watson were not in each other's company again until late in the fall. High school was over. There were no school events to pull them together and her father's rules about the boys she could date was a wall Jordan wasn't permitted to climb, so the summer passed. At the university, though, there were no nuns around, and her father's gaze didn't extend to Lexington.

There was a sorority mixer. Her sorority.

Jordan had been invited.

Whether he knew it was her sorority or not is unclear, and whether his invitation was issued at her suggestion isn't recorded.

He was standing by the punchbowl, scanning the crowd and waiting for something to happen when a voice whispered laughingly in his ear, "Game?" Immediately he knew. Sue.

That's when it began in earnest, neither of them realizing it at the time.

They enjoyed each other's company. They liked the same books, the same music, shared a voracious curiosity, had offbeat senses of humor, a wide circle of mutual friends, and an urge to be together as often as time and circumstance permitted.

By the time their senior year came, they were on the brink of something serious.

There is no way in the natural order of things that this could have been avoided.

That he and Sue Watson were seeing each other was no secret on campus. Several of Sue's Frankfort classmates were in her own sorority and she was friends with others. Word found its way quite eagerly back to that office on the second floor of the Farmers & Merchants Trust Company building.

He was not a martinet, Andrew Watson, though he had that reputation in some circles.

He was firm. Yes. Definitely. Some would say rigid, even demanding.

Men who put money at risk expecting to profit from the transaction have to be firm and demanding. This is not always understood and often generates a degree of dislike among those whose entreaties are declined or who hope to get relief when certain debts come due and do not.

Set those considerations aside, and he is otherwise a pleasant man—good company, outstanding citizen, a generous supporter of worthy causes. His wife is well liked, his children handsome and well behaved. He is a pillar of the church, his church, the Holy Roman Catholic Church, its most prominent catechist, and boon to the community. But firm. And demanding.

Understandable, Jordan would be nervous as he sits waiting to be ushered into the presence of the most powerful man in town.

He is greeted with a smile and handshake.

Andrew Watson is a big man, firm grip, wide smile. Friendly. Working in his shirtsleeves. Informal. Welcoming.

Confusion adds to Jordan's nervousness. He had expected Mr. Watson to be suited, sitting behind his desk, sternly authoritative, ready to pontificate. Imperial.

Instead, it's "Sit down, boy. Thanks for coming in. I knew your father. Fine man."

He motions Jordan to a chair bedside his desk and moves around to take his seat behind it.

"You are about to graduate."

"Yes, sir."

"Plans? Graduate school? Straight out into the job market? Something in sight?"

"I had thought about law school, sir, but find I'm more interested in writing than in arguing. I've taken some courses in journalism and like the freedom that offers me. I think I'll try that."

Watson sinks back in chair, folds his hands across his stomach, seems to be considering the idea.

"Not much money there," a slight, dismissive nod. "You would do well with the law. I imagine one or two of the big firms here would be interested in bringing you aboard. That could result in a very good life here. Rewarding and satisfying. But you have other plans. I wish you luck."

Leans forward then, still smiling, though, "Now as to the matter of Sue."

"Sir?"

"I'm told you're something of a couple. I talked with Sue about this when she was home last week. I am disappointed, but she is no longer a child, and [he can't keep a note of pride from creeping into this voice as he says this] she has always been of an independent mind."

"Yes, sir," is the only reply Jordan feels bold enough to offer.

Watson folds his hands again and sits back studying Jordan.

"That's all you have to say?"

"We have been seeing each other, yes. And yes, sir. She does have a mind of her own."

"You knew I preferred she restrict her dating to boys of her own faith?"

"No disrespect was meant. We were good friends. That grew into something more."

"I want it to end now."

"Sir?"

"I want you to go away. I want her to start developing relationships with young men suitable to the life she is meant to lead. Young men of her own faith."

Watson stops here. He lets Jordan marinate in the thought. Then resumes in a voice of absolute finality.

"The only way your relationship with her can continue is if you convert to Catholicism and are baptized into the faith."

The unexpected demand stuns Jordan. The force of it almost takes his breath.

"She won't resist me in this. As a girl sampling life, this little diversion with you for a while is permissible, perhaps. But as woman with a life to lead and a family of her own in time to consider—no. She won't resist me in this."

Watson pauses, waiting for a reaction. Anger? Fear? Guilt? Surrender? When there is none, he rises, walks around the corner of the desk to look down on Jordan still seated and still speechless.

"You will never be a true believer. To pretend to be would be worse than sin. It would kill your soul and savage what little self-respect you might have left. I don't think you are willing to pay that price. I don't think you should pay that price. End it. Tell her. Lay it on me if you like. But end it!"

Then, "Good-day, Mr. Aimes. Thank you for coming to see me."

Thus was Jordan Aimes dismissed.

WEDNESDAY, SEPTEMBER 19
Day Twelve

"Yes, I remember," Cal says again, eyes still not leaving Jordan's, passing him the flask again. "It was a hot day. You left the door open. I told you to close it, you were letting the flies in. Then you told me your story."

Jordan was bedraggled. The combined forces of anger and embarrassment, mingled with recognition of his weakness in the presence of power, had drained him. He was limp and spent.

"When you finished, I asked you what you intended to do. You said, 'I don't know. What should I do?'"

"Do you want to marry the girl?"

"It hasn't gone that far."

"Do you want to?"

"I don't know. Maybe."

"Are you willing to pay the price the father demands?"

"No!"

"Would she be willing to defy her father?"

"I don't know."

"A man who marries young gives hostages to fortune. He takes on responsibilities that shape his life. I read that somewhere."

"What does that mean?"

"When a man's only responsibility is to himself, his freedom is limited only by his ambition and abilities. When he takes on responsibility for others, he no longer has that freedom."

"What are you telling me?"

"Watson has done you a favor."

Later that night. Back on campus. Walking through the dark with Sue.

"Your father…

"I know. He told me."

"Is he right?"

"Yes."

"I thought…." he says.

"I thought…." she says.

Neither finished.

What was there to say into the silence that could make a difference.

"He's done you a favor, that's what you told me."

Motioning for the flask back, taking it and capping and sliding it back into the pocket in his fishing vest, Cal stands and stretches, turns back to Jordan.

"Watson gave you your first taste of what real power is like. You've been reacting to that ever since. And he took away the hostage that you might, to your regret and hers, have given to fortune. He did you a favor. A bigger one than I think you realize."

"There was something else you told me."

"Which was?"

"You said listen. You said there is a little voice always whispering in your ear. Listen to it," you said. "That's your essence talking."

"I said essence? I used a word like essence? Should have said gut. That's primal. That's you. Listen to your gut."

It's still light enough to move about, but carefully, perhaps another twenty minutes or so to dark. Off toward the creek, fireflies are beginning to play. There are fears that they will become extinct, doomed by the chemicals farmers are using to protect their crops and the urbanization destroying the meadows and the creeks where they live. Be a pity to lose them.

"It's getting dark. Why are we talking about this?"

THURSDAY, SEPTEMBER 20
Day Thirteen

First light is at six.

Calum's house is on the creek. Most of the Macklin land is on Elkhorn. Rich bottom land for crops and haying. Prime pastures for livestock. Calum's house is on the ridge above the dam on the north creek just above the Forks.

The house is a modest one-story with a sleeping porch so that in summer you can be lulled to dreamland by the whisper of the creek, and a big front porch with swings and rockers.

They've been talking all night.

Not exclusively about Jordan's Rubicon, but mostly about that, on the porch for a while, then inside around the fireplace as the night chill rose and whippoorwills sang.

Now with the sun rising, they're in the kitchen, Jordan's situation explained, his options understood.

Give them credit for control. Cal is a sentimental man, a caring man. If you've heard his music, you know it's so. Jordan's dilemma distresses him mightily, but he has not let his anger or his sorrow seep out.

And Jordan has kept his ache and his apprehension controlled. He needs to be strong in the face of this affront. Pity or sympathy would derail him. Whatever hand fate deals you, don't bitch about it. Don't whine about it. Deal with it. That's what's written in that little book Cal had him start.

Cal is busying himself with getting breakfast made. He's not married, so there is no wife about. Jordan has been out on the porch watching the sunrise. They're both still running on adrenaline. You remember the energy—the all-nighters before big tests at school, the parties that kept going somewhere til daylight.

They're on the edge of exhaustion now, but not quite. And not talked out. They've managed, at least in their conscious minds, to strip out the anger, the fear, the outrage and are weighing the options—rationally, they think.

To Calum Macklin there is no option. He plays poker like he owns the deck, does his own handicapping at the races. He understands how to weigh the variables that produce wins. There are no variables here. No nervousness to catch in a man's eyes when the pot is large and the bet is raised, no stud line to tell if your horse has the blood to win in the stretch. Nothing but chance here. And no odds to compensate.

There is still the question. Jordan asks it.

"What would you do?"

Cal is standing at the sink drying his hands. Biscuits are in the oven, ham in the skillet, eggs waiting. He stops. Straightens up, turns around to be facing Jordan.

"If you risk the surgery and it is successful, the pay-off is a long and happy life. If it isn't successful, you'll die on the operating table or be left a cripple. There are three possible outcomes.

Only one of them good. If you don't risk the surgery, death for sure. A month, maybe two. But death anyway. So they say. What if they are wrong? They're not likely, but what if they are? What if they don't know for sure? Helluva gamble. The odds are against you, but everything you're looking at is a helluva gamble. What I'd do is fold my hand and go look for a fairer game.

"This is the only game in town."

"I know," Cal says, "I know."

"The death part doesn't bother me that much. The other does."

"I know," Cal nods. "Would me, too."

He finishes with his hands and drapes the towel on its hook.

"How lucky do you feel?"

They sleep into the afternoon.

Wake. Wash up. Make themselves presentable. Make sandwiches and chase them with Bloody Marys on the porch.

For a night so filled with consequence, their conversation is relaxed and easy. But guarded, as if they are reluctant to raise the ghost of that discussion. Instead, they talk of yesterday's fishing, and Cal's music, and of family things.

"I think there is a song in last night," Cal says.

"I want credit for the best lines," Jordan replies.

Cal hums a bit of a tune, "A start. What do you think?"

"Nice, very nice."

"Make sure you hang around long enough to hear it all."

Jordan smiles.

Jordan's grandmother, his mother's mother, when he was a small boy, used to put him to bed with a story when they visited the farm. She would then kiss him and tell him to sleep well, that his guardian angel would watch over him through the night.

Mamaw was an Edwards, not a Macklin till she married, and ever after, still. The Edwards blood is as thick as the Macklins and the family name as old.

And she was, of course, like the Macklins, a Baptist. The Baptists populate the valley of the Elkhorn.

They believed such things then, things like guardian angels and the devil on the prowl. Many still do.

Jordan grew up being taught such things. He outgrew them. But like everything we are taught when we are young, little vestiges remain caught in his mind and come popping out at unexpected times, sometimes in dreams, but mostly when there is a hard decision to be made, a path to follow of which he is unsure.

Cal grew up believing such things, too. He didn't outgrow them.

Maybe that's why his music is so sweet.

FRIDAY, SEPTEMBER 21
Day Fourteen

Jordan has talked with the Colonel and with his uncle Calum. Still wants to see Aunt Maggie, talk with Billy.

And must talk with Danny—Dr. Daniel Andrew Moran, Chief of Neurosurgery, University of San Francisco Medical Center. How much time does the good doctor need to set up the surgery? A day? Two days? Must be a complicated affair— a team to assemble, instruments to gather, an OT to schedule. Not like a visit to the ER. Must talk long with Danny. He'll lose a day each way going back to San Francisco. He doesn't want to waste two days on airplanes, but he wants to know exactly what they plan to do and how they plan to do it, he wants to be walked, step-by-step, through the whole procedure so that he has it fixed in his mind, understands where the risk lies, know exactly what he's betting on.

He will have to go back to San Francisco. A day to get there, a day to get back, a day for asking and listening. Three days, then. Say three days for that. Which means he needs to make his decision by the end of the first week in October to give Danny time before Date Certain arrives.

The moon is dark that week. Ah, but the stars shine brighter when the there is no moon.

Friday is laundry day.

He is in a life-or-death labyrinth looking for a way out, yet the ordinary still must be attended to. Always. Everywhere.

His wardrobe here isn't much—a blue blazer, a button-down white dress shirt, grey slacks and a rep tie, khakis, jeans; some polos, several long sleeve Orvis fishing shirts spiffy enough to be worn under a jacket, a blue sweater, a necessary complement of socks and undershorts. No pajamas. He doesn't sleep in them. No robe. He dresses immediately when he rises.

There is a full wardrobe in his apartment in San Francisco, from tux to boardshorts, but here he expects no demands more formal than an evening at the club, which the blazer and the button-down will accommodate. The polos and the khakis are respectable enough for whatever casual social encounters he may find himself in.

He hopes to avoid those. Not many have bought the Honest Dick Tate explanation. It's assumed he is working on something important. He's been away too long to have been brought back purely by nostalgia. Out of politeness, people aren't pressing him. But some soon will. The curiosity is too intense. Those closest to him will. Tom Andrews. Cindy, when she let's go of Honest Dick Tate. TJ definitely.

Jordan doesn't want his situation to become a matter of general conversation. Or speculation. Or sympathy. The thought that others might find him an object of sympathy is a humiliation not to be borne.

So he's on his way to the laundry with all this rattling around in his mind when the text alert sounds on his iPhone.

Jordan glances down. This is Tom. Get to me fast.

There were no skid marks to indicate excessive speed, no scorched rubber on the pavement to say he was braking hard. A sunny afternoon, not a cloud in the sky. Nothing at all to explain why TJ Browning's pickup crashed through the barriers on the curve at the overlook on Bald Knob Pike. There is a magnificent view there, out over the ridges of the inner-Bluegrass, and an eighty-foot drop into the rocky gorge below.

Took the rescuers over an hour to free him from the wreckage and bring him back up the cliff.

He wasn't much alive then.

He isn't now.

They've kept him in the ER. He is too fragile to move.

Jordan is there. Tom Andrews is there.

Mrs. Browning, Sue, she isn't. She is in Lexington shopping. They've managed to get word to her and she is on her way back.

Tom knows the doctor. They're talking outside the room. Jordan is inside, standing beside TJ's bed, holding TJ's hand, more a comfort to Jordan than it can possibly be to TJ, but he must do something to cushion the hurt.

When Tom comes in, he shakes his head. "Nothing they can do. He's too broken. He'll go soon."

Finally, Jordan lets go of TJ's hand, lowers it back down onto the bed.

"TJ. What have you done?"

The shock of it shakes the town.

TJ Browning was well known and well liked. Fine family. Important man in state government.

A pity.

It was thought he may have had a heart attack, or a stroke, some unexpected shock that caused him to lose control. How else to explain it?

So young. In his prime. So sad. A pity.

The talk dominates the dining tables.

Wasn't there something about a drinking problem?

Gossip, only gossip. He was a fine man. Will be missed.

TJ died before Sue could get there.

He did not die unaccompanied. Jordan and Tom were there. They took some comfort in that. And then they waited for Sue.

By the time she arrived, TJ's body had already been taken to the mortuary.

They took her there and sat with her until family gathered and close friends arrived.

If comfort can be had at such a time, when the shock is still numbing and the fact of it not yet fully registered, they were there for that. There was nothing more they could do. They said what little they could say, held her hand, kissed her on the cheek, and left.

To Tom's.

Anna already knew and is waiting. It had made the eleven o'clock news.

She meets them at the door. No words. The looks they exchange are enough. She shepherds them into the den, has the fireplace lighted and the room lights bright. Soft music in the background. The sound of utter silence would be too much.

They settle, the three of them, lost in thoughts of yesterdays, lost in their own other times, letting their tensions release and the fatigue leak away.

Jordan is the first to break out of it.

"Remember the Winchester game," he says to Tom. "TJ tackling the ball-carrier right into the coach, knocking the bench over and spilling the players out onto the field. All of them scrambling trying to get up. The whole crowd laughing. Stopped the game. We gave TJ the game ball."

Tom smiles, "He was so proud he kept it in his office sitting on a tee."

This is the first smile that has crossed either's face since the afternoon. It doesn't linger long.

Anna, sitting quietly, listening, knows there is no comfort she can offer. They were boys together. There is something special about that. Some bond that forms and lasts.

Maybe it's the way they play together, testing, teasing, seeing who's strongest or fastest, or toughest, the way they seem to be constantly competing with each other, yet supporting and protecting. Maybe it's the things they experience together as teammates, the pride they feel and the closeness.

She thinks it is fortunate for the species that girls become women and leave behind girlish ways. Men do not do that. They become men, but they do not outgrow the boy within them. She finds that charming and endearing and comforting in some men. In others she finds it threatening and frightening. At the very least, disappointing.

Hoping to lift some of the gloom, Anna decides to intervene.

"Enough. It's after midnight. Time for a nightcap and then bed. There will be time enough tomorrow for grieving."

They start to stand when Tom suddenly jerks upright.

"Well, I'll be damned." He turns to them. "I will be damned. He did it on purpose!"

His action takes both Jordan and Anna by surprise.

"He drove off that cliff deliberately."

The next few minutes are a jumble of questions and confusion that none of them remembers clearly, only the excitement of it, until Jordan asks the obvious question.

"Why would he do that?"

"Because," says Tom, "they can't indict a dead man."

Jordan and Anna stare at him in amazement.

"It just came to me. Sit down, sit down. I'll get the drinks. Sit down, I'll explain."

And they do.

And he does.

Brandy for Jordan. Brandy for Tom. A long-stemmed Riedel with chardonnay for Anna.

They stay seated. Tom remains standing. Holds his glass out to them. They raise theirs. "TJ" he says. They repeat it, mystified.

And lift their glasses and complete the ritual.

It is the saddest and bravest story Jordan has heard.

Don't call it suicide. Suicide is too crass a word for what TJ did. A man could take pride in what TJ did. And the way he did it. And why he did it. The discipline, the courage that took— you had to admire that.

Anna has moved them out of the den and into the kitchen.

They're sitting around the table, putting an end to the evening. They've talked through it all, let their emotions run. They are sad and despondent and downhearted and blue. Pick any adjective you like. Yet, they are relieved. And, in a strange way, proud.

Jordan and Tom anyway. Proud of TJ showing such courage. Proud of his sacrifice to save his family so much pain.

There is anger, too. Anger at the men who drew TJ into their web.

Anger at TJ for letting them.

Dammit, TJ!

Dark outside. Morning almost.

"Long run out to your place on the creek. Plenty of room here. Stay. Get some sleep. Don't make that drive in the dark."

"Yes, Jordan," Anna says, "please stay."

He's tempted, but declines.

At the door he turns back to Tom.

"Nothing we could have done?"

The possibility that there might have been gnaws at Jordan.

Tom knows this, knows Jordan, a half-smile forming on his weary face, verifies. "Nothing."

SATURDAY, SEPTEMBER 22
Day Fifteen

He didn't make it to the laundry.

It was completely forgotten, would not have come to mind today except he wakes remembering that he will need a jacket and tie for the funeral.

He's not sure when that will be. Soon. The Catholics don't prolong these things.

The first funeral he ever attended was Catholic, a friend of his father's, in the white church downtown. He was only six or so. He remembers how strange it was with the bells and the incense and the sunlight streaming through pictures made of stained glass where windows ought to be.

And the bloody body nailed to a cross hanging over the altar.

That frightened him.

He bored into his mother's side for comfort.

But the music, the music was grand, organ and voice, filling the silence. The ritual made him think of spells being cast.

He doesn't remember exactly what he felt. He does remember feeling he was in a very strange place and that something very scary, very odd, was happening. And that he did not want to be there.

He does not want to be at the one upcoming.

And hopes to avoid his own if he guesses right.

Stay out of it, Jordy, he tells himself. You have no role to play. She has all the support she needs. You're a dim memory from a distant past. Pay your respects. Offer your help if it's ever needed. Stay out of it.

Yet…

She once was a true love of mine.

The melody and the words are stuck in his mind, that and the thought. And TJ was a close, close friend. Can't pretend not to care.

Ah, Jordy, Jordy, you don't have time for this.

Tom calls just before ten.

"UK's playing Mississippi State today. I have tickets on thirty, 30th row, best in the stadium."

"So?"

"Pull your head out of the doldrums and get with the program. I'll pick you up in about an hour."

"What's going to happen?"

"We're gonna win."

"No. With the Grand Jury."

"You think I'm wrong."

"I think you know more about football than you know about law."

Tom's right. UK does win, 21 to 7. Sends Ole Miss packing and keeps the hopes of the faithful alive that the Cats will earn a bid to a bowl at season's end.

And he is right that the maelstrom of the game would help snap Jordan out of the funk of TJ's dying.

Jordan is laughing and joking and fully into the game-day high as he and Tom walk back across the campus. They both are. No way to be down on a day like this. Your team wins, you're engulfed in a crowd of happy, festive people, it's a perfect autumn afternoon. Golden, absolutely golden.

So, two for two for Tom. Right about the game. Right about Jordan's mood. Is he right about the Grand Jury?

"Are you?" Jordan gives word to the thought as they walk.

"Am I what?"

"Right about the Grand Jury?"

Tom stops and looks around and sees a green bench sitting beside the walkway beneath a splendid autumnized maple.

"We'll know Monday," he says, propelling Jordan toward it.

There are others on the walkway, coming and going, little groups of two and three, a single now and then, attractive young students in bright sweaters and scarves, sport-jacketed alumni, casually dignified as befits maturity and station, and in the distance, back across the campus, the sound of the band still playing. They have privacy enough there. No one takes notice of two middle-aged men resting for a moment amid the fallen leaves in the afternoon sun.

Tom sits down, pats the seat beside for Jordan to join, shakes his head good humoredly, "We're on the campus of the famous University of Kentucky on a glorious September afternoon. Our team has just won an important game. We're on our way to gloat and sip a dram or two of the Commonwealth's best with friends and teammates in the hallowed confines of the Faculty Club and you've got dark thoughts weighing you down. It's too nice a day for that."

Tom sits back, looks around, turns back to Jordan.

"For a District Attorney to bring an indictment and seek a trial, he must have a defendant. And that defendant must have the right to a trial by a jury of his peers—the right to confront his accusers and to defend himself. That's impossible if the accused is dead. You can't indict a dead man. There may be some gossip, but nothing in the press. No public naming. No public shaming."

He slaps his hands on his knees, stands up, says with finality, "TJ will get the outcome he wanted. Be glad about that. He paid a big enough price. God's in his heaven, all's right with the world."

SUNDAY, SEPTEMBER 23
Day Sixteen

This is a dream.

I'll wake up shortly.

I'll be in my own bed in my own room. I'll feel good. I'll feel strong. I'll feel eager for the day and what it might hold.

None of this will have happened.

No Danny. No TJ.

When I wake it will be a grand, bright morning with fog fingering under the Golden Gate.

I'll wake soon. I'll pull on some shorts and head out for a run.

It will be like it was.

And this will all be gone.

Jordan is coming awake in the cottage by the creek ... not in his own bed, not in his own room, three thousand miles back to San Francisco.

Not like it was ...

All of it still here.

OK. All right. Better awake than in that dream.

If he could pick a time, it would be the day before Danny's call, that day on the North Platte.

He was fine then. Happy then. Had his game together. Felt fine. Had Liddy. Had things to do he loved. No complaints. Lots of laughs and hurrahs.

If he could go back...

...if.

Get your sorry ass up. Deal with it.

Sunday.

Sunday morning go to church, family there.

Macklins and Edwards by the carloads. Aunts and uncles and cousins. Slide in beside Aunt Maggie. The feeling of them all there together, sharing their care and their certainty in that little church by the Forks.

Singing.

How he loved that. All those voices blending together.

Believing. Caught up in the promise.

Hear Billy preach. Hear him, so passionately and so convincingly assure them that they are loved and cared about and that all their pains and cares will be lifted if only they stay faithful, if only they believe.

Ah, well.

No. Don't go. Cause too much stir. All that hello-ing, and look-who's-here-ing, and what-a-grand-surprise-ing.

Too much commotion.

Would be a sumptuous feeling, all that welcome and affection pouring out, but no, don't go. Don't intrude on Billy's show.

The creek, then. Sun's out.

Elkhorn's running clear.

Pack a lunch and fish up creek—Church's Grove, Hawk's Hole, King's Hole—then back down for the one's he missed. Get the beer he left cooling in the water at the hole where he went in when he wades out.

Find a nice soft rock to sit on and watch shadows get the water ready for the night.

By himself. No one to listen to but himself.

No one requiring attention but himself.

No sounds but the sound of water over stone and night birds, calling. That whole little world of creek and solitude, his alone.

Elkhorn Creek meanders through the heart of the Bluegrass.

The North Fork rises just east of Lexington and flows 75 miles through Fayette and Scott counties. Lexington is the home of the University of Kentucky and many of the world's most famous horse farms. In antebellum days, Lexington was known as the Athens of the West, it was that sophisticated. Much of that charm retains.

The South Fork rises west of Lexington and runs 52 miles through Fayette, Scott, and Franklin counties.

The two streams meet east of Frankfort and form the Main Creek, which, in turn, flows north into the Kentucky River at Strohmeier's Camp, a run of about 18 miles.

That's 147 miles of stream flowing through some of the richest agricultural and most beautiful countryside in the land.

Calum's place is on the South creek, just above the Forks. The Macklin home is on the North creek, east of the Forks along the Georgetown Road. The cottage Jordan is renting is on the Main creek near Knight's Bridge—just to make sure you're oriented.

The stretches Jordan plans to fish are on the main creek. He's going to wade them, not float them. Those who aren't addicted to a flyrod won't appreciate the distinction. Stepping into free-flowing stream with a flyrod in hand and the water running clear is like slipping through the looking glass into another world—a peaceful, comforting world where nothing but the setting and the cast are worth attention.

That's where Jordan needs to be today—no TJ, no Sue. No Danny impatient for an answer.

On Elkhorn. There has to be a trophy smallmouth lazing behind that big rock at the foot of the riffle at Hawk's Hole. Has to be. Cast up above. Make sure the Coachmen settles on the seam as gently as a falling leaf, mend to adjust the drift so that there is not the slightest hint of drag.

Be ready for the strike.

Don't glance away.

Be ready.

No fish is so fine a top-water fighter, none more combative. Hang a hook in his lip and he'll come to the top and try to throw the lure right back at you, not retreat to deep water and wallow around. Inch for inch and pound for pound, the fightingest fish that swims, the prince of the freshwater gamefish—the smallmouth black bass.

On Elkhorn. On a bonnie autumn afternoon. No TJ, Sue, no Danny.

Supercalifragilisticexpialidocious.

MONDAY, SEPTEMBER 24

Day Seventeen

If Jordan's life were a three-act play, Act I would be about his time here, the growing-up-and-learning-things time.

Act II would concern itself with the starting-out-and-making-of-a-career time.

Act III is the one he's writing now. It begins on the North Platte with Danny's call. How it will end is unknown. Much, maybe everything, will depend on how successful Dr. Danny and his team are with the surgery, if Jordan opts for it. Or on Billy's God, if he's paying attention.

Ought to make the decision. Quit delaying. Give Danny as much time as possible. Do the medicos practice this sort of thing, rehearse it, the surgery? Surely, they must.

Cal says it's all pure chance anyway.

Why not just flip a coin?

The Grand Jury convened at ten, made its report, and was dismissed with thanks for their service shortly before noon.

The big news was a human trafficking indictment against a Louisville society doyen and a criminal attempt at tampering with a witness in a Pikeville murder case.

There was nothing concerning fraud, no mention of bribery in the awarding of a state contract.

There had been heat at the time, conversation and speculation, especially among the reporters whose beat was State Government, but when asked about it in the press conference afterwards, the District Attorney said there was no charge to be brought. Irregularities had been noted. The winning bidder of the contract in question had been disqualified and the contract awarded to the runner-up. Next question.

No indictment.

No names.

No one pressed it.

Rest in peace.

Anna has the charcoal started, the steaks coming to temperature, the wine breathing, and the Eagle Rare out and open when Tom and Jordan arrive.

The funeral is tomorrow. Tom and Jordan are to be pallbearers.

She has taken special care to dress for mood—a yellow cashmere cowl-neck sweater for fashion, bright and happy. Designer jeans for casual informality. Anna is an attractive woman. And smarter than she wants you to think.

She and Tom were married the day after their graduation from college. Jordan did make that one. He was Tom's best man.

Tom Andrews, Thomas Quincy Andrews, is a man of consequence.

That might not have been obvious in references made so far. Tom's company writes the insurance for most of the state's major corporations, plus its professional sports organizations, several universities, and carries just under forty percent of the state government's contracts. His contacts are wide, his influence considerable.

This was not to be expected when he and Jordan were boys. There was never any question about how bright, or aggressive, or energetic Tom was. The question was would he self-destruct before his assets had a chance to be put to play.

Tom partied too hard and drank too freely—only beer then, but too much. He was good at almost everything he tried and never had to try very hard. Except at sports. He gave everything he had in every game and to great effect. He led them to the conference championship their senior year.

The thing was that he was so much fun, and such good company, and so ready to lend a hand, that he was just naturally a winner hatching. Everyone knew it.

Anna knew it.

And when they began to date in the summer before their senior year at college, when she finally gave in to his annoying entreaties just to shut him up, Tom Andrews started becoming Thomas Quincy Andrews.

Tom and Jordan were the best friends then and are best friends now, never mind time and distance, and tomorrow they'll walk to the freshly dug grave of their good friend TJ Browning carrying his body between them.

Don't want to think about that tonight, Anna thinks, think of other things—of shoes and ships and sealing wax, of cabbages and kings.

"What?" says Tom, mystified.

"What?" says she, startled.

"Cabbages and Kings?" Tom demands.

"The Walrus and the Carpenter," Jordan breaks in, delighted with the rhyme, "and why the sea is hot. And whether pigs have wings."

"Pigs? Wings? What the …"

"Oh," she laughs, "I was thinking out loud. I was thinking that tonight we are not going to think dark thoughts. We are going to tell stories and repeat gossip, the good stuff Jordy hasn't heard, and play good music and maybe get a bit high. Not enough to have a head in the morning, but enough to feel good. Tomorrow's load is for tomorrow. Tonight, is for tonight. Don't just stand there."

TUESDAY, SEPTEMBER 25
Day Eighteen

It is a good morning for a sad day—a bright morning, cool and crisp with frost still on the ground in the shadowy places. Birds are calling. The sun is shining.

The funeral is at ten, in the little white church downtown, the one where the broken body hangs on a cross above the altar.

Tom and Jordan left at nine to join the four other pallbearers at the funeral home. Their charge is to lift the casket with TJ inside into the hearse and ride with it to the church and stay with him all the way.

It is an honor to be asked to carry your friend to his grave.

When they reach the church, they'll take the casket from the hearse, Tom and Jordan at the head on either side, and carry TJ down the center aisle to his place at the foot of the altar.

The church will be full. There will be music, organ and choir, promising and comforting. After the ritual of the service, they will carry him back to the hearse and ride with him to the cemetery.

There they will lift the casket again and bear it from the hearse to the open grave. The path they'll have to follow is uneven, a rise to climb and downslope to master. Fallen leaves are everywhere, some obscuring the path, some slick underfoot. The casket is heavy. They must not stumble or falter. This gives them something to set their minds to rather than to the burden the are carrying. All these men were boys together. They'll be remembering as they walk.

When the casket is in place, the family will be escorted to seats in a row alongside. Mourners will gather 'round. A passage will be read. Ecclesiastes perhaps: For everything there is a season, and time to every purpose under heaven. Jordan doesn't know this to be one of TJ's favorites, but it is one of his and would be a comfort this particular morning.

There will be sighs and tears. And pangs of loss. And prayers said.

And silence.

Then Thomas Jonathan Browning will be laid safely down.

It is a sad day for so good a morning—bright sun and blue sky and birdsong in the trees, yes, indeed, a good morning for so sad a day.

Back at his cottage later that afternoon, Jordan stands on the porch in lonely silence, considering.

To spend a day so close to death, to walk to an open grave, to watch the casket lowered into the ground, shouldn't he be downcast or despairing? Considering his own situation, shouldn't he be?

That he isn't surprises him. And pleases him.

Maybe he really isn't afraid. Maybe.

That thought has his mind, that and his conversation with Tom.

As is the practice, close friends of the family had been invited back to the Browning home after the funeral—a wake of sorts, but after, not before.

The ingathering helps ease the family past their shock and their loss. They tell stories, remember good times, shed tears if they must, but in the hugging and the laughing, and the just being together, the gloom begins to diffuse.

Tom and Jordan have been mingling, wandering from one small cluster to another across the big back lawn to the tables on the patio loaded with food and drink. They've been making small talk and reminiscing. Everyone is processing the fact that TJ is dead, that Sue is a widow, and they are wondering how she will fare and how their close little world will change.

She is holding up remarkably well. She has her emotions in hand. Her manner is strong. She has support. Her father is retired but is still a power, her mother and her sisters are close by. She and TJ have no children, but friends aplenty. Anna is among her closest. There is a group around her now. Anna is there.

Jordan and Tom have found a bench beside a big old oak at the far end of the lawn with a rope swing hanging from its lowest branch. The kind of swing they played on when they we were kids.

No kids.

What does that say, Jordan wonders. TJ? No. Sue's sister's children? That must be it. Sue has it for them.

Why no children of her own?

Jordan has been uncertain about how to approach Sue. More uncertain about what to say. Most uncertain of all as to what he wants to say.

Strange things happen when the past comes back, when the past steps out of time and into your arms, her cheek against his as they danced that recent night at the club with TJ beaming. When the past comes back what was becomes what is. And feelings that have been asleep begin to come awake.

It was so long ago he probably isn't remembering it right.

Is he?

They both stepped away from it.

Didn't they?

They are different people now.

Aren't they?

Ok, Jordy, get a grip.

You've fantasized and romanticized, and it was nothing like the picture in your mind.

Yes, you both did step away from it—reluctantly, sadly, disillusioned, but deliberately.

And yes, you are very, very different people from the girl and the boy who thought they were on the edge of something worth having all those years ago.

Jordan: "She'll be alright?"

Tom: "Sue? She is a strong woman. She has plenty of support. There will be no money problems." He glances across the lawn to Sue. Anna is with her and Cindy has just walked up. An embrace, a kiss, something said that he cannot hear, and then a subdued smile on all their faces. Something remembered, something fond or funny. Keep it light. Keep the anguish at bay.

Jordan has followed his gaze, watches as the women talk.

"She and TJ, they were happy?"

Tom, watching too, caught up in the women's instinctive urge to comfort, says, "Happy enough, I guess. Until the end. TJ's drinking was a problem."

"No children?"

"Anna says there was some sort of complication. They tried doctors. Nothing worked."

Jordan nods, stands and stretches, walks over the swing. Looks to Tom, a questioning smile forming. He tests himself against the ropes, presses down on the wooden seat. Smiles again, sits down, pushes back… and is swinging.

"Backward, oh backward turn time in your flight. Make me a boy again, just for tonight," Jordan says, laughing delightedly. The women have caught the motion and are watching, too, and laughing. So is Tom.

This is totally inappropriate for so solemn an occasion, Jordan realizes. He had no intention of attracting attention or intruding on the mood of the afternoon, just the urge to be that free again. But everyone's mood has seemed to lighten. That can't be bad.

He stops. He's feeling so good it's difficult to remember what it's like to be down and offers his seat to Tom. But by that time Anna is there insisting it's her turn. And the afternoon segues into a party.

He left without talking with Sue about what he thought he might talk about. The day was going too well for that. She kissed him on the cheek. He could not read what her eyes were saying.

On the way back to Tom's, the one question he could not keep from asking: "Why did he do it, Tom, the contract thing? What could cause him to do that?"

Anna is driving. She has been their chauffeur all morning, taking them to the funeral home to begin the day and then carrying them from the cemetery to Sue's after the funeral. Tom is in the front seat with her, Jordan behind.

Tom leans back across the front seat, "Money maybe. A ticket to the Big Boys' club. TJ wanted to start moving in those circles. It would have played to his ego. Shelby was also on that board, not a mover and shaker, but wants to be. He may have been the one who enticed TJ."

"Our Shelby?"

"TJ had to be brought in by someone he trusted. Someone who knew him well enough to know how to play him. Shelby is the only one among the organizers who fits that description."

"Not Shelby. He's a 2nd Street Irregular. A pallbearer. Not Shelby."

"Shelby."

"He bears no responsibility, faces no consequence?"

"Their company pays a fine. The board members walk away."

"That's all?"

"Nothing to do, Jordy. If you go after it and open it up, you'll bring TJ right back into the center of the whole mess, create exactly the public circus he died to prevent. Leave it alone. The moving finger has writ."

They're pulling into Tom's driveway. Jordan's car is parked to the side.

"Not supper time yet. Come in for a drink. Stay and eat," Anna says.

"Tempting," Jordan says, "but I've got to pack. Off to San Francisco in the morning."

"You're leaving?"

"I'll be back. And Tom, our Shelby—the Piper always gets paid."

WEDNESDAY, SEPTEMBER 26
Day Nineteen

No direct flights from here to there. So he gets an early morning from Lexington to Dulles, catches a United direct from there to SFO and will be on the ground a little after one, the three-hour time-break working its wonders. He should be in his condo in the Oakland hills before two-thirty, no tie-ups on the freeway into the city and just ahead of the afternoon traffic turmoil on the Bay Bridge.

He has not called Liddy.

He'll be a surprise. A welcome one, he hopes. Call her when he gets unpacked. See about drinks and dinner.

He has already called Danny. Yesterday. Made arrangements to meet him in his office at the Medical Center at ten tomorrow morning. Get the full run-down. Meet the team. There is a team, he learns. That's reassuring ... sort of. Reassuring to know he's going to be in the hands of an elite team of surgical wizards, a little menacing to realize that what they plan to do requires so many of them.

He'll save the rest of the day and evening for Liddy, then head back to home base the following morning.

Do not waste time. Get this settled.

Twenty-five hundred miles. Five-and-a-half hours. He's crossing the whole girth of America, sea to shining sea, Atlantic to Pacific. Depending on the weather, he'll be able to watch it unfold. He always does. The magnificence of the land never fails to mesmerize him, and the grit and determination of the men and women who opened it up and stitched it together amaze him. O brave new world, that has such people in 't.

Come on, Jordy, spare me your quotes. Look out the window if you like but concentrate on your quandaries.

Danny deserves a decision.

Liddy. There is Liddy. What are you going to do about Liddy?

And Sue. All at once she's back in your life and you're uncertain of what that might mean.

And Shelby. What to do about Shelby.

You don't have time for all this, do you?

Five hours to touchdown. Get at least some of it out of the way.

Jordan is riding first cabin.

It is a conceit he acquired early in his career working for a CEO he much admired. If I can't go first class, I'd just as soon not go, that CEO told Jordan, and he ran his business on that principal: If we can't do it first class, we won't do it all. They were always first class.

The man also abhorred standing in line to spend his money—concerts, shows, events, restaurants. "I wouldn't stand in line to get into the Last Supper," he'd say if presented with one, and they'd move on. Jordan didn't know whether that was impatience or ego, but he thought it a noble ambition.

Later, when Jordan left that privileged world and descended into the melee of competitive journalism, he took whatever transportation he could get and stood in as many lines as necessary. But given the option, Jordan Aimes goes first class. And, though he does not stand in lines, he would make an exception for the Last Supper.

He had a love affair with San Francisco once.

It's over.

The high-tech hoards have bought its soul. Its streets are littered with the homeless. The traffic is impossible. The ambience phlegmatic.

Yet its charm remains. At night, from the deck of his condo in the Oakland hills where he lives now, watching the city sparkle like a jewel on the ocean's edge, with the cable cars climbing and the fog coming in, at night the fairy-tale city still emerges.

He has not gotten any of it out of the way.

He is no further along on Danny or Liddy or Sue, or how to get the Piper paid, than he was when the wheels went up on the flight from Dulles.

One thought melds into another and segues in a third and meanders out into jumble of intertwined problems with so much consequence to each that he gives up in frustration and decides as a matter of sanity he must take his little quandaries one at a time, block out the others, focus on them One-At-A-Time! Which he will not be able to do. They all have urgency. Ah, well.

Liddy was not there when he called. He left a message.

Dinner on his own, then, which is OK. Jordan is not bored in his own company.

Trader Vic's tonight. The original Trader Vic's in the alley in San Francisco is gone now. The one in Emeryville on the bay does nicely and it's only a short drive away.

A Fog Cutter to start.

Then Crab Rangoon, followed by a serving of Bongo Bongo soup, followed by a heaping Crab Louie with extra dressing. Then two scoops of vanilla ice-cream bathed in caramel sauce with an almond cookie.

But only black coffee to chase. No cognac or brandy. Still that call to Liddy to make.

"You're here," she says when he says her name. All he has said is Liddy. How does she know that?

"You owe me dinner. Why didn't you call?"

"How did you know I'm here?"

"My people are from Umbria. We have magic."

"Black?"

"White. Be careful. The other can be called upon if necessary...and Danny told me you were coming."

He laughs. "Ah, Liddy, I've missed you."

"Then pay me that dinner you owe me."

"I have Danny tomorrow. Could take most of the day. Tomorrow night. Any place you like."

"Meet me at The Bourbon and Branch. Five-thirtyish. We'll go from there."

"Done."

Out of the bantering now, concerned. "Are you okay?"

Lydia Bacarro fascinates him in surprising ways.

She is not for standing around wringing hands when trouble appears. She's for looking monsters squarely in the eye and kicking their butts. This is not a quality of character properly raised young Southern girls admit to, girls like those Jordan grew up among, though many of them do so with unremitting satisfaction while smiling demurely and not soiling their Ferragamos.

Lydia is not Southern. She's San Franciscan—San Francisco Italian, by way of Umbria. Her forebearers in that little village at the head of the valley where the mountain roads crossed turned Hannibal back and saved Rome for a time. Some genes travel well.

She is classy beyond compare, compassionate and caring, but absolutely intolerant of foolishness or self-pity, and unapologetically so.

As tall as Jordan.

Hair black as midnight.

Eyes emerald green.

A contralto's voice. A body buff.

She will comfort him, but not coddle him. She will take his hand and lead him to the door and stand ready to help him through—the door she knows he should open, the door she wants him to open. If it is another, she will still be there to piece together the aftermath.

"Are you okay?" Not bantering now. Tender.

No. Maybe. I don't know. All of these run through his mind.

What he answers is, "When I see you, I will be."

THURSDAY, SEPTEMBER 27
Day Twenty

Thursday, September 27, 2018. Sunrise is at 7:02, sunset at 6:59.

The high will be 64 degrees, the low 52. The moon is waning gibbous.

Expect low clouds and periods of light rain most of the day, but clearing toward evening. It is a rainy, misty morning. Low clouds and fog, the bay barely visible.

The Kavanaugh Supreme Court confirmation hearings are underway in the chambers of the United States Senate in Washington (contentious and inflammatory).

United States Secretary of State Michael Pompeo is on his way to North Korea to make arrangements for a much-heralded historic meeting between President Donald Trump with North Korean Supreme Leader Kim Jong-un (highly controversial).

Jordan Aimes is to confer with Dr. Daniel Andrew Moran, head of the Department of Neurosurgery, University of San Francisco, and his team, at the Medical Center in San Francisco, beginning at 10:00 a.m. (fraught).

Traffic will be terrible, the Bay Bridge choked by the morning commute, the city streets clogged. Getting across town to Parnassus Heights once he makes it off the bridge will stretch all his patience. He wants to be at the Medical Center by nine-fifteen at the latest. Forty-five minutes to find a parking spot and get in. He loathes being late.

How to dress for a meeting with the wonder workers? Jordan likes thinks of them in this way—a cabal of wizards ready to do their magic for him.

He has taken particular care. First impressions make a critical difference. Is this a person of importance or a cipher? Is he to be taken seriously or can he be safely ignored, a winner or a loser? Dress is key to this.

For today something subdued and professional, something suitable to the seriousness of the occasion, but relaxed. A blue blazer, a white button-down with a wine-colored tie, neatly creased grey slacks, cordovan tassel-loafers freshly shined. Yes, Jordan worried about his shoes being shined all those years ago for his meeting with Banker Watson. Made no difference then, but Jordan felt freshly shined shoes said something important about a person's sense of self. May make no difference now. But he still feels this way.

Sunshine and blue skies would be preferred this morning. Better omens. There is some comfort in the fact that the Medical Center is in Parnassus Heights. In Greek mythology, Parnassus was the home of the Muses and the favorite of Apollo, the god of healing and music, of prophecy and the sun, and Dionysus, the god of wine and ecstasy. Not that Jordan is superstitious, but if Apollo and Dionysus are on his side, not to worry.

Danny is waiting.

Dr. Daniel Andrew Moran, late of the 2nd Street Irregulars, Head of the University of San Francisco Department of Neurosurgery, is waiting, standing in the entrance lobby, hands on hips, all eager and welcoming.

"Nice place you've got here," Jordan says.

"Wait until you see the surgery," says Danny, grinning like the Cheshire Cat in Through the Looking-Glass.

They both laugh, bear-hug despite the decorum of the spacious lobby, and walk off together past the entrance desk into the interior.

The team is assembled in a modish windowless conference room with whiteboard walls and a large built-in projection screen at the far end.

There are six. They are seated at a long rectangular table of highly polished wood, three on each side, a chair for Jordan at one end, for Dr. Moran at the other. Three men, three women. All in white lab coats. Very professional. There is no levity in the room. No warmth. Deadly serious. (Bad word choice.) Intently serious.

If what they plan to do is successful, they will make medical history. Jordan hadn't considered this, considered the feelings of men and women committed to his plight. Immediately he feels better. They have an incentive beyond merely saving a life. They are gambling their reputations on this.

Even so, he would like to sense a little warmth, a little feeling of connection.

Danny introduces them each, details their credentials, experience, specialties. They are all, of course, beyond impressive.

Jordan traverses the table. Shakes hands with each one, says thank you to each, looks into the eyes of each, seeking that connection, the understanding that this is more than doctor to patient. It is you to me. Connect.

The presentation begins then, with Danny leading.

They walk him through the complete procedure, step by step, from the moment he arrives to the completion of the surgery, explaining what is to be done at each stage, why it will be done, and how it is to be done.

TV animation shows him how the procedure will unfold, pictures the aneurism and its position in the brain, shows how they will get to it and remove it. And how his recovery will unfold. Elapsed time for the surgery, four to seven hours. Recovery time from the operation, four to six weeks.

The closing visual shows the team unmasked, arms in air, smiling broadly. Would make a nice poster.

Afterwards in Danny's office—"Well?"

"Remember Cal, my uncle Cal?"

"Sure."

"He said never play poker with a man called Doc. Don't draw to inside straights. And do not bet longshots... unless you're sure they'll win."

Danny smiles, nods appreciatively.

"I know. It's hard. But you have to decide. Soon. The longer we delay, the greater your risk."

"What would you do?"

"You've met the team. You've had the procedure explained. The precautions we'll take to ensure that it is successful have been discussed and the simulation reviewed."

"You'll be the one with the instrument in hand?"

"I will."

"It's a longshot, Danny."

"Life is a longshot, Jordy."

He considers that on the drive across town to meet Liddy. And agrees.

And decides not to think about it any longer.

From Parnassus Heights on the edge of Golden Gate Park down to the Marina ought to take 20 minutes max. At this hour, with people heading for the bridges that will take them out of town he'll be lucky to make it on time.

Doesn't want to be late. Wants to be waiting at table when she walks in. There is valet parking at Bourbon and Branch. Chalk one up one for the good guys.

And so he is.

Lydia Bacarro has a thing about punctuality, too. She is never late for things she has agreed to. Late is an insult. Ladies are late only on purpose.

Jordan is standing by their table with a glass held out and smiling as she approaches.

"I ordered," he says.

"So I see," she says, "Blanton's and branch?"

"Eagle Rare neat."

"Well, well," she laughs, "it has been awhile."

A kiss hello.

And down they sit.

Already he feels lightened. Literally. There is an air about her so reassuring that he almost automatically feels comforted. He came away from Danny's not in a dark place, but somber— reassured by the knowledge that some of the finest surgical talent in the country is on his case, but doubly aware that chance is the hunter and he is the prey. Liddy's presence dispels those thoughts.

A lovely woman who likes and wants to help you, bright lights and happy people, a fairytale town with nothing in store but warmth and understanding. Let the good times roll, Jordy, ole boy. Let the good times roll.

FRIDAY, SEPTEMBER 28
Day Twenty-One

Liddy was not happy when he left.

Cocktails at Bourbon and Branch went fine. And dinner on the waterfront at Scoma's in Sausalito was finer. A window table, the view back across the bay to the city sparkling in the night, the wine. And abalone, they had fresh abalone. Golden.

Until…

"Are you close to a decision?"

She had shown remarkable restraint throughout the evening. The conversation had been light and laughing, nothing of particular consequence, friendly lovers word dancing. He knew it is the matter most distressful in her mind. She'd let it lie until now.

They were almost alone in the room. Only one other table was occupied, and it was not near them. The lighting in the room was subdued, dimmed as the night progressed to give the view across the bay more sheen, the flickering light of candles on tables providing the only luminescence, except for lights at the bar and they were low.

They were on coffee, letting the evening wind down in its unharried way. He reached across the table and took her hand.

"A very wise man told me to never make a decision before you have to. If you make it too soon, he said, you may make it not knowing all you need to know in order to make the best one. But don't wait too long. Time or changing circumstances may take the decision out of your hands."

"Yes?"

"Not yet. I'm not there yet."

"Your session with Danny didn't reassure you?"

"It was impressive. The team is impressive. The sophistication of the procedure is impressive."

"But you're not impressed?"

"I am impressed."

"Why can't you make the decision, then?"

"There is something I still don't know that I want to know."

"About the procedure?

"No, Liddy. About me."

He is airborne out of Oakland on a six-thirty a.m. flight to Frankfort via Chicago to Louisville. Hertz the rest of the way.

Didn't want to fight the morning traffic getting across the bay and across town and out to SFO. Oakland International is closer to his condo by almost an hour. Should be at the cottage on the creek by five—the three-hour time change working against him this time.

Four hours to Chicago, two down to Louisville. Two more to get to the cottage. Eight hours, assuming the weather is okay, the connections connect, and he doesn't have a flat tire or crumple a fender. Be there by five.

In the meantime, nothing to do but read. Or watch the country unfold beneath and the clouds float by outside. Or think.

Jordan has never been particularly introspective.

He does not spend time examining his feelings or his motives. He has never felt the need to "find" himself. He's not confused or unsure about who he is.

But now he wonders. Should he be? Is that why he's here? To find if there is a him he is unaware of?

And then he laughs. Aw, come off it, buddy. And holds his cup up for the stewardess to refill.

Liddy, though.

He's unhappy with himself for leaving Liddy as he did last night. She is so clearly concerned about him and he's given her no comfort to ease her anxiety. If she could make the decision for him, she would look that monster of doubt squarely in the face, kick its butt, climb on that table, and tell Danny to do his best. As a partner in a successful venture capital firm, big gambles are her forte.

He knows she wants him to take the gamble. She has not said so. Would not say so, even if he asked. The decision must be his alone, uninfluenced by others. She knows that. She feels that.

If he gambles and wins, they can walk off hand-in-hand, a happy couple forevermore … if they are of that mind. He has the feeling she might want that. He might, too.

If he dies on the table, she'll see he's properly laid down.

If he winds up with worst of all possible outcomes, she'll see he's taken care of and his dignity preserved.

Whatever happens, she will be there.

Liddy is a treasure. He must not mislay her.

SATURDAY, SEPTEMBER 29
Day Twenty-Two

He doesn't recognize the car.

Jordan's only visitor has been Cindy Vail and she's not been to the cottage since she moved him in. Who has come calling so early on a Saturday morning? The sun isn't even over the ridgeline yet.

Breakfast is done. The dishes put away. The coffee pot's full. The place is neat. He can be neighborly.

Why he is in a neighborly mood escapes him. A good night's sleep, no dream residue tainting the day, the morning looking happy and inviting—he wakes that way sometimes now, used to be most of the time, feeling good, feeling really good, feeling friendly. Like today.

He watches from the cottage window as the car comes down the lane, mildly curious, but with no idea of who it might be. A new Jeep Wrangler. Steel Grey. (He had a Grand Cherokee once, red. Good car.)

Would not be neighborly to make a visitor climb the porch steps and knock on the door. The neighborly thing would be stand on the porch waiting to welcome whomever, whatever.

So he steps out into the morning as the car pulls to a stop and a young man gets out.

He's tall. Slim. Not much more than a boy. Twenty perhaps. Not older. Caucasian. Doesn't look like a local, dressed too well for a Saturday morning. Hair too neatly combed.

"Good morning, sir."

There. The accent. Doesn't recognize it. Slight, but distinctive. European? Definitely not a local.

"Good morning. Beautiful morning. Are you lost?

"You are Mr. Jordan Aimes?

"I am."

"I am not lost. I came to find you."

"That's interesting. How can I help you?"

A personable young man walking around the car to stop at the foot of the steps to the porch where Jordan is standing.

"My name is Tate, Norris Tate. I hope I can talk with you. About an ancestor."

"Yours or mine?"

"Mine, sir. His name was James William Tate. He was born near here."

"Sorry. I don't know a James William Tate. Or know of him."

"I was told you are seeking information about him. Honest Dick Tate I think he was called."

Honest Dick Tate? Jordan gives the young man a closer look. Neat. Clean shaven. No visible tattoo. Polite, respectful. Where this one came from he can't imagine. Honest Dick Tate. Please.

Jordan laughs, "Who put you up to this? Playing jokes on a Saturday morning. Tom Andrews? Well, come in. Come in.

The coffee's hot. I can't wait to hear the story you two have concocted."

Norris Tate is the son of Hanson Tate of the Estancia de la Tesoro of the state of São Paulo in Brazil. The 100th anniversary of the birth of the patriarch of the Tates of São Paulo, James William Tate, is approaching, he tells Jordan. James William is buried here. Norris has been sent to inspect his gravesite and the stone. To see that it is intact, and that stone is still legible.

The Brazilian Embassy in Washington arranged his documentation and transport. His great-grandfather came on the same mission for the 50th anniversary. Every fifty years one of the Tates of São Paulo will make the pilgrimage.

"Honest Dick Tate is buried here?"

"Close by."

He wants me to believe this? Honest Dick Tate's vanishing act and likely whereabouts is still one of the biggest mysteries in the history of the state.

Jordan laughs and shakes his head in disbelief.

"That's an incredible story!" He pushes his chair back and applauds.

"Bravo. My compliments to both you and whomever else is in this with you. Tom Andrews, I imagine. You can tell Tom you had me hooked for a moment. And you, you did this very convincingly. Earnest, sincere. Very well done. You've made my morning. Thank you."

He means that sincerely. His past few days have been flooded with melancholy. Some levity is like a panacea. Suddenly the morning has become more interesting than he had any hope it might be. He leans forward, fully engaged and interested.

"Who are you? How did Tom find you? That slight bit of accent, the way you're dressed. You're not from here. An actor. That must be it. A student actor. UK? Transylvania? What's he paying you?"

"No, sir. Please. What I told you is true. Please. I'm not playing a game. I have no idea who Tom is."

The young man is so distressed and so sincere that Jordan almost begins to believe him. He likes the young man, but he can't credit the story as true. Too many experienced people—police, detectives, reporters, bounty hunters—have spent too many years trying to find Honest Dick Tate not to have found him, especially if he was hiding in plain sight.

"I will show you. I will take you to the site. You must promise to keep it secret. I will take you to the grave and you can see for yourself."

"If this isn't a charade, why are you here?"

"We learned in the Embassy that you are writing a book about James William Tate. His reputation here, we know, is bad. At home, he is esteemed. He is honored. For the life he led and his achievements. We want it to be known here that the last half of his life made up for the first half of it. Through you. Through this book you are writing. That he was a good man. An honorable man."

"I'm not writing anything. I'm merely considering."

"We understand. We have the documents that you need. His journal. It is very candid. It covers everything—from the transgression to his final days at the Estancia. You will see when you read it. You must come to the Estancia. His works in São Paulo will speak for themselves when you see them."

"Who is we?"

"The family council. The council is in unanimous agreement. Will you come with me to see the grave? You will know I speak the truth. You will know you must tell this story."

I don't have time for this, Jordan thinks.

But, oh my God, what a story. Solve the Honest Dick Tate mystery after all these years. Unravel the saga. If the answer is there for his having, how could he stomach not knowing? Dammit, I don't have time for this.

SUNDAY, SEPTEMBER 30
Day Twenty-Three

They are to meet mid-morning. Norris will pick him up. It's on the way. The road ends at a trail. They will need the Jeep.

"But we will have to walk some, over rough ground. Dress accordingly."

Jeans and running shoes will have to do. He has nothing more suitable with him.

The farm is west of Peaks Mill, on an isolated stretch of the South Fork. If ever it was a working farm, the farmer had to be a marveldon to make a living off it.

The boundaries of the property are fenced and look in good repair, the fields mowed, dried stalks waving in the breeze in a field where corn was grown. A forgotten little piece of land attracting the attention of no one except the farmer contracted to tend it.

Jordan is feeling more foolish by the minute. What a ridiculous story. Interesting. Inventive, but ridiculous. He expects Tom Andrews to jump up any minute laughing. He's tempted to call it game over, but keeps following Norris, who walks ahead, a small backpack over his shoulder and a rake in his hand, fully intent on his mission.

At the far end of a small meadow, above the flood plain, there is a stand of white oaks aglow in autumn colors. Norris leads him there. They are stately and old, three of them spaced randomly, but close enough that their canopies keep the clearing in shade most of the day. Inside the clearing, the ground is level and free of understory.

Inside the clearing, a small wrought-iron fence frames a space near the far end. The fence is tall enough to discourage cattle, but low enough a man can step over.

Inside the fence, a long rectangular slab of polished granite lies on the ground. There is an inscription on it. The young man motions Jordan to come closer. It reads:

James William Tate
Born Franklin County, Kentucky, 1831
Died São Paulo, Brazil, 1919
Here He Lies Where He Longed To Be

They both stand silent. Not even glances are exchanged.

There is a little wind, enough to make a slight whisper in the trees. Nothing more. The rustle of leaves and the hum of breeze. The lonely quiet of abandoned country.

Oblivious to Jordan now, Norris begins to inspect the site. He checks the fence and finds it firm, kneels to look closely at the inscription on the stone, carefully runs a cloth over every word to make sure it is crisp and the letters distinct, then carefully polishes the length of it.

When he has finished, he rises, steps back over the fence and into the clearing, and with the rake, begins making it neat, making it look cared for, removing debris the wind has blown in, excising the understory that might later prove intrusive.

Realizing the importance of the moment to the young man, Jordan has tried to make himself as invisible as possible, of no more note or notice than the oak he leans against watching, feeling almost reverential himself, as the young man moves slowly to the foot of the grave and kneels.

The young man kneels there, closes his eyes, lifts his face to the sky. Whatever he has to say he says for ears that hear only thoughts, for he says nothing aloud. Then he bows his head and clasps his hands in the posture of prayer, and does.

It is as touching an act of honor and homage as Jordan has seen.

When Norris rises, he looks around, seems then to remember Jordan, finds him against the oak, nods only, starts back across the field toward the car.

It is a reflective ride back to the cottage. They do not talk. When they are at the cottage again and Jordan is getting out, Norris says only, "Do you believe me now? Will you come? Will you write the story?"

Jordan doesn't answer right away. He opens his door, gets out. Leans back in though the open window. They are face-to-face, eye-to-eye—he with this young man with the fantastic story, and the young man with him—the man who can tell the story he wants told.

Jordan is impressed by the young man. Thinks he's honest and sincere.

He doesn't realize the risk he's running, Jordan thinks.

If I get really into the story, the hero that the Tates of São Paulo have created might not survive it. Might be best to leave the patriarch unexamined and Honest Dick Tate still hidden in the folds of time?

Jordan likes the young man. Send him home with as much accomplished as the Family Council could reasonably have expected. Let him enjoy the congratulations and the rewards of having made the trip and planted the seed.

Will he come?

One more thing to add his bag of burdens. A gem of a story, an important story, a story for the ages.

If he lives.

If Danny's untried operation is successful. If he decides to risk it.

Will he come?

Don't think about that now. You've got enough to think about.

You can think about it if you bet the longshot and it wins.

But never bet a longshot. That's Cal's rule. Never bet a longshot unless you're sure it will win.

Who could possibly know that?

Of course.

Billy's God.

Billy's God is in charge of all things— is all powerful and all knowing.

Sunday night service at the church at the Forks. Billy will be there. It is his church. He'll be preaching.

Jordan remembers how much he liked those services when he was a boy, the warmth, the music, the feeling of being in the midst of a big, happy, caring, family.

They know. They're sure. Jesus loves me, this I know, for the Bible tells me so. That's what the song says. He even remembers the tune.

Why not go? Wrap yourself in some of that certainty. Slip in a little late after they're all assembled, attract no notice, create no stir.

Go, be comforted.

On Sunday mornings while he was still a boy, he went to Sunday School every week, dressed in his best Sunday-go-to-meeting clothes, on orders to keep them clean.

Then to church right after, and home or to Aunt Maggie's for Sunday dinner.

Every other day of the week, dinner was the nighttime meal. On Sundays, dinner was right after church. It was the big meal of the week. Sometimes the preacher came, almost always an aunt or an uncle with their brood. And more a happening than meal, a half dozen or so friendly people telling stories and cutting up. And the food. No one set a finer table than his mother or Aunt Maggie.

By mid-afternoon nearly everyone was satiated and mellow and had left for their own homes to get ready for the Sunday night service: Seven-thirty, rain or shine.

Until he had reached the age when he began to think for himself about the stories he was being told, it seemed that he and his mother never missed the Sunday services, morning and night. He didn't object. The music was good. The ritual reassuring. And the knowledge that he was wrapped in the arms of a big caring clan favored by the Almighty gave him a warm and buoyant feeling.

He misses those Sundays. Those days, that feeling. Sometimes. Even now.

The service has started by the time Jordan gets there. He can hear the hymn all the way across the road from the little parking lot beside the creek. Lights are already on in the church. Outside, twilight is giving way to dark. He should be able to find a seat in a back row. Attract no notice.

Billy is standing in front of the pulpit, singing, smiling. He has a fine baritone. He sang lead in their boy's quartet. Tom was the tenor.

The Reverend William T. Newall—B.A., Georgetown College; M.Div., Duke University; Ph.D., Southern Baptist Theological Seminary; Pastor, Bell's Grove Baptist Church, the church they both grew up in. Billy, now the Pastor. Think of that.

Jordan's connection with the Reverend has been complicated. Billy wasn't one of the 2nd Street Irregulars. He was a year ahead of them in school. So there was that senior-to-underclassman ego edge to navigate. They were teammates in some things, the debate team, the choir, football. And competitors in others, for grades, for elective offices, for girls. Through it all they developed a grudging regard for each other and even, though they would not use the word then, a liking. Their careers took them on different paths, but they kept in touch, and they were friends.

Jordan left when the closing hymn began, slipping out unnoticed. It was full dark then, a waxing gibbous moon just over the tree-line.

Billy was good. He always was. He is so sure that what he is telling you is right and true, and he tells it so well, that even the great unwashed willingly suspend disbelief. For a while at least.

At least for as long as the glow lasts.

Feels good, Jordan decides.

Feels like one of those Sunday nights so long ago.

MONDAY, OCTOBER 1
Day Twenty-Four

Never mind the autumnal equinox. Fall doesn't get here until October.

All the leaves have turned by then. The hills are painted, and the neighborhood streets are canopied in color. The town and all the surroundings are a kaleidoscope of scarlet and orange and yellow and brown. There is excitement in the air. Fall is here, and he's on his way to Billy's.

They both moved away. Jordan chasing his dream. Billy, too. But they never really left. Billy missionary-ed for a while, bringing the Good News to the Horn of Africa, saving souls in the Balkans. He was a very effective young missionary, handsome, articulate, energetic, caring—a man to keep your eye on.

The church hierarchy moved him back to the States, brought him to headquarters in Louisville to groom for bigger things. He was a comer. He was going to be a star. Whether he did something they didn't like, or they did something he didn't like (bet the latter), the Reverend William T. said thank you, no, and came home to shepherd the flock at Bell's Grove.

True, it is a small church, but it has a proud tradition and there is no flock more ardent this side of the Pearly Gates—just a little country church sitting in a meadow by a creek, the kind of church that men who work the land and with the seasons build for themselves and their families. There are stained glass windows, a proper steeple, and an ancient bell to call the faithful to worship.

Billy is in his study there. Jordan knows the way.

The last time they talked face to face was three years ago.

Jordan was in town for a few days following his work on the meth-in-the-mountains story. A Sunday. Billy would be preaching. Jordan went. Not because he was a churchgoer, but because he wanted to hear Billy.

Billy could make you feel that angels really did have your back. Or that hellfire was licking at your heels. Watching Billy at work on a Sunday morning was better than front-row-center at the best morality play on offer. There was no better way to spend a Sunday morning than with the Reverend William T. Newall in the pulpit and all the sinners listening hard.

"You never fail to transport me," Jordan told him after the service.

"You never fail to derail me," Billy said with delight when he saw it was Jordan. "Sinners run down the aisle eager to be saved when I offer the invitation. But I never seem to be able to get you out of your seat."

The congregants leaving the service flowed politely around them, smiling at the two men, their pastor and a man who seemed familiar, but they couldn't quite place, so obviously enjoying themselves.

The pastor's study is in the vestry at the rear of the church. There is nothing pretentious about it. It is comfortable—a desk, some chairs, a wall of books, some pictures, an old cast-iron wood-burning stove for the winter days when it's cold, and windows, big ones, on the east wall and the west wall, giving the room a barrage of natural light on good days, and a moody hue on others; a sanctuary where fine sermons can be fashioned and secrets heard and protected.

This day is one of those days when the big window on the west wall is letting apprehension in. It's cold and grey outside and a misty rain wets the window. Not to Jordan's liking. What he's come to discuss may prove depressing enough without the help of the elements.

The Reverend, though, doesn't seem bitten by the day and is as warm and welcoming as anyone might wish him to be. He has a nice little fire going in the old stove in the corner and has just set a crystal decanter filled with an amber liquid on the edge of his desk.

"Back in the day it was muscatel, remember," he says, lifting the decanter and holding it to the light.

"It was all we could afford, sitting around the fireplace those rainy nights at Kitty's, pontificating on everything and enjoying every minute of it. Cognac seems more fitting now. Remy Martin to your taste? I keep a little on hand for special occasions. The sun's almost over the yardarm. Let's drink to us. To you, to me, to all of them. Whatever happened to those boys," he says, smiling at the picture in his mind. "Iechyd da!"

The thought and the phrase catches Jordan.

Those boys.

What did we think we'd be those rainy nights so long ago? Captains of the Universe. Governors of the Planet Earth.

Jesse's dead, blown into pieces too small to collect by an IED as he led his company into Baghdad. Bruce overdosed in Memphis chasing the dream that wouldn't come true.

Danny is in San Francisco, an accomplished surgeon and head of a leading medical research institution. Tom is here, successful, a pillar of the community.

I'm here, for now.

Those boys. They were worth the price of admission.

It is a very good cognac.

They take their time with it, laughing over the things they did, the pretentions they held, catching up on time lost and people remembered. A warm time. The mood in the room lightens for Jordan as they talk, so he finally has the nerve to broach what brought him here.

They've talked before about what he wants to talk about now as young men around campfires on cold nights when the deer had been invisible the live-long day. They toyed with it over late-night beers after college parties, showing off their pretentions at erudition and poking holes in accepted truths.

But it was play. Billy wasn't the Reverend then.

Jordan wasn't a man with his own demise in sight.

It wasn't serious then.

What Jordan wants from Billy now is to understand why he is so certain that what he says from that pulpit is true.

He wants to hear it from Billy, not from the Reverend William T. Newall, not from a man who has the burden of a doctrine on his back and a credo to uphold, but from the person he has known since boyhood and for whom he has respect. Not Pastor to congregant. Billy to Jordan.

Billy has just finished a story about his time in the seminary, a funny story. He pauses, smiling.

Jordan says into the pause, "I have eight days to live, give or take a few."

Billy rocks back, frowning in surprise, not sure he heard what he thinks he heard.

"Say again. Live?"

But Jordan goes on, "I have an inoperable brain aneurism. It may kill me in a week. Danny has an untried surgery that might save me if it's successful. If it isn't, the surgery itself will kill me or leave me a vegetable after a massive stroke."

"My God," Billy says, shocked almost into speechlessness, "you're serious."

"Danny found it. I'd been having headaches. I never have headaches. He examined me. Found it."

"He thinks he can remove it without killing you?"

"He thinks so. But the surgery has never been tried. It is purely experimental."

"The eight days?"

"Danny figured the aneurism might hold for a month or so. The month is up in eight days."

"What are you doing here? Why aren't you on the way back to San Francisco?"

"I'm here because I wanted some questions answered. I have one for you."

"Anything, Jordy. Tell me."

Almost reluctantly, Jordan asks it: "What comes next?"

"Next?"

"Heaven? Hell? Nothing?"

"Oh, Jordy, damn, how can anyone know that? I didn't know when we were playing those arguing games and I don't know now. I don't know, Jordy. I didn't know then and I don't know now."

"Then how can you tell people the things you tell them from that pulpit every Sunday. Tell them and want them to accept it. Tell it so earnestly that they do."

"Because I believe it. I believe it to be true."

"But you do not know it to be true."

"We're only poor little creatures, Jordy, specks of carbon in an infinite universe of wonders and mysteries that are beyond the reach of our understanding. These things that I talk about from that pulpit, that I talk about every day to anyone who will listen, are in that space. I can't prove them to be true, but that so many of us believe, and have believed over the centuries, is proof enough for me."

"Why do you believe it?"

"Because I choose to."

"That makes it true?"

"I was told long ago that the most important decision I would ever make is what I choose to believe. This is what I decided to believe. I have never regretted it."

Jordan's turn now to sit back, to study Billy's expression, to work over what he said. No epiphany. No voice from above on the road to Damascus. Only a belief. Not a truth. One that he decided to embrace. A decision.

"Then what do you choose to believe happens next?"

"What I believe doesn't matter. The thing that matters is what you believe."

There is silence after that.

The two of them sit there, wondering.

A virgin gave birth to a boychild.

That child was God incarnate. He cast out devils, performed miracles, caused the blind to see and the lame to walk, raised men from the dead and promised life everlasting if only you would believe in him.

He was crucified by the Romans as an insurrectionist seeking to overthrow the Emperor, died on the cross, rose from the dead on the third day, ascended into heaven and will come again.

Jordan is of the opinion that there has to be a prime mover, a force—a god, if that word works best for you—but The god, not one of the many gods running around through history looking for worshipers to follow them, the one that is omnipotent and omniscient, who created this universe and all others—the capital-G God. The Deity.

He believes this because anything as complicated and precise and simple and beautiful and terrifying as this little slice of it we have can't be accidental. Just looking around is proof enough. For a being with such power anything should be possible.

A virgin birth? Of course.

Raise men from the dead? Absolutely.

Walk on water? Piece of cake.

Did it really happen?

There is no question in Jordan's mind about the primal force, the prime mover, the capital-G God.

But the rest of it?

To be taken on the word of men who say they've talked to God, who say God has spoken to them and revealed his intent, who say they have had ecstatic dreams and seen glorious visions and been told how we are to conduct ourselves and the rules we must obey, and know this because it has been revealed to them, what is good and bad, what is true and false—men who profess to know the mind of God.

Of this, Jordan is skeptical. All that he is sure of is what he does not believe.

When Jordan leaves Billy says, "it's a matter of surrender, Jordan, surrendering your ego."

The rain has stopped. Dark soon.

TUESDAY, OCTOBER 2
Day Twenty-Five

Jordan has examined the places and events caught in his memory, felt the joy and the hurt again, summoned to mind the people who left their mark on him. He has tallied up the account of who he owed and for what, sometimes ached over what he should have done, but didn't, sometimes shudders at what he did, but should not have done. And smiles at the remembrance of things he should not have done but did anyway.

How does it tally, he wonders?

Whatever he is looking for is still unfound.

Sue? Is that what he left here?

The life that he might have had here had he stayed, is that the treasure lost?

Billy's God?

Me?

Is anyone keeping score? Does any of it make any difference?

Seven days.

For the past few hours Jordan has been driving the town again. Slowly. Looking for what is there that was there when he was young. And conjuring up what isn't out of the pictures in his mind, as if there is a door that would let him back through time, and if he could find it, he could slip through it and be home again, and safe.

He is on the lip of the hill above the old quarry now, sitting on the hood of his car, leaning back against the windshield. There is a country lane leading up to a grassy turn-out across from a cornfield where the farmer backs his harrow around. From it the whole valley can be seen—from the dam by the distillery all the way up-river to the bend beyond the Capitol and across the valley to the beacon light on the cliff at the cemetery on the eastern rim of town.

He used to park with his dates after dances up here. No one else seemed to know about it. He didn't share it. It was his. On full moon nights it was a place where fairies danced. There is no moon this night, but the sky is cloudless and Orion sparkles on the ridge line.

What has he forgotten that he needs to remember?

He told Tom this morning. Laid it all out.

He had not planned to. Not this soon. He intended to tell Tom, of course. His hesitation was not out of concern for Tom's feelings. It was his own ego. He could not stand the thought he'd be felt sorry for.

He was at Tom's office on another mission. The Piper that led TJ to that cliff had to be paid. They passed a few happy hours running through all the appealing options that sprang to mind, from kneecapping to tar-and-feathering, but in the end he accepted that there was no civilized way to make this happen.

So Shelby Crittenden, of the 2nd Street Irregulars and longtime friend, would walk away at the mercy of only his own conscience, which had so far proven nonexistent. And their scorn.

They agreed that each, separately, would arrange to meet with Shelby and read him off, make certain that he knew that they knew, and held him beneath contempt.

Would he care?

Perhaps not, but the respect of those you grow up with is indispensable to any man's sense of self, and though Shelby was unlikely to feel lesser of himself, to know that others whose opinion he valued did, would be a lingering pain to his ego.

"Who first," Tom said. "You or me?"

Which opened the door for Jordan to bite the bullet and tell Tom.

"To get with Shelby? Better be me. I have a time problem."

"You're not running off to San Francisco again."

"Not yet," said Jordan, and then he told him.

Tom's eyes never left Jordan's as he listened. He sat quiet and still through the whole recitation—the diagnosis, the odds, the options. And remained quiet when Jordan finished, his eyes never leaving Jordan's face, but seemingly unseeing. The brain does that when the spirit is stunned. It disconnects the synapses between the mind and the emotions, short-circuits the connections, lets the facts register, but freezes the feelings.

Jordan knows. He froze his when Don told him he was dying.

Don was several years ahead of them in school, but he was as fast a friend to Jordan as any but Tom. They had bonded over words Jordan's sophomore year, Mrs. Smith's class in the prose and poetry of England.

It was the poetry that got them. They found themselves seduced by the words, by the rhythm and the rhymes, by the pictures in their minds their interplay created, by the emotions they stirred. They were soon committing whole poems to memory, competing in little duels of first lines and whose verse is this. Which grew into a wider friendship of books and music and eventually escapes to Elkhorn with flyrods when they could find the time.

Don became an academic, a professor at UK's School of Journalism & Communications, which they both attended. Don made his career there, Jordan headed off to the waiting world.

They had gone to lunch that day at a favorite restaurant on a corner just off the campus of the university, a regular event when Jordan was in town. Don was on a cane when he came through the restaurant door, but other than an initial look of surprise on Jordan's face and a dismissive smile on Don's, neither made a thing of it.

They told stories and laughed, reminiscing, no mention of the cane, no talk of the scars of passing time, no wonderings about what might be coming. Thanatos not named. The Pale Horseman ignored. Stoicism was their style.

When it was time to leave, Don said, almost matter-of-factly, "I'll say goodbye now. I won't see you again. I'm dying."

He was barely in his forties.

Surely not.

But it was surely so. They did not see each other again.

Jordan had no words of comfort for his friend then. Nor thanks for their long and happy friendship. He regrets that to this day. But still does not know what he could have said or should have said.

Except to rage at fate.

From Tom, leaning back in his chair behind his desk as if distancing himself from a disturbing happening, only a hooded stare as he digests what Jordan is telling him, filtering the facts from the backwash of emotions, packaging the revelation as a matter to be dealt with, not to commiserate over—the default position that puts feelings on hold and allows us to react calmly, show the strength we should. As Jordan had done that day with Don.

"Seven days?"

"Danny thinks it will hold for at least a week or so."

"He could be wrong."

"And I could be run over by a truck as I leave here or hit by lightning out of a clear blue sky."

"Are you scared?"

Jordan takes time to test that in his mind, decides, "Not yet."

"Anything you want me to do?"

"What can you do?"

"Whistle Dixie?"

It's such a funny, unexpected response that it jars Jordan out of his doomsday mood. And he laughs. And Tom does. And the morning is not quite so dark.

Relieved now, the ogre out in the daylight where it can be seen and sized and looked in the eye, Jordan feels better—the thing revealed, the challenge understood, a true friend knowing and standing ready, Jordan feels immeasurably better.

"Have you decided?"

"Not yet."

"You're pushing it awfully close."

"I know."

"So?"

"One more door to open. I'm doing that tonight."

"And then?

"No more doors. I'll have to decide."

"Do I have this right? You have an aneurism in your brain that can burst at any minute and kill you dead on the spot. But Danny has a surgery that can save you if it's successful?"

"Or kill me if it isn't."

"What's to decide? At least with Danny you have a chance."

WEDNESDAY, OCTOBER 3
Day Twenty-Six

The cemetery in Frankfort is called the Westminster Abbey of Kentucky.

It sits on the eastern rim of the valley where the town is nestled. The Kentucky River flows below, winding through it in two graceful arcs and glistening like a ribbon of silver on nights when the moon is full.

There is no place more peaceful on God's green earth. And few as beautiful.

Jordan is on his way there now to find a place to lay himself down.

Which he may need soon. Depends on how the coin lands when he flips it.

Whenever that time comes, he wants to lie in home ground. Not among strangers in strange lands, but among family and friends, alongside people he knows.

The Superintendent of the Frankfort Cemetery Company is Roger Goodman. With time fast running out to Danny's deadline, Jordan is meeting with him this Wednesday morning.

He and Goodman, a tall, lanky, engineer type with a surveyor's eye and a storyteller's trove, will tour the parklike grounds and inspect the available sites. The cemetery has been accepting lodgers for over one hundred and seventy years. Many of the most desirable plots are occupied. So Jordan needs to look thoroughly and choose carefully.

He will want to know where the sun will set when daylight ends and where the moon will rise when night begins; what trees will shade him on summer days and blanket him in color when autumn comes.

He'll want a clear view of the sky to watch the clouds form and play, and a clear view at night to track the stars on their way. And grass all around. And far enough removed from the road and the paths that harsh sounds won't intrude to sully his mood.

Much to consider, much to weigh.

Ah, Jordy, Jordy. It is no small thing to pick the spot in which to spend eternity.

Roger Goodman is pontificating for Jordan as they walk from where they've parked near the little chapel down the path to the Daniel Boone monument.

"Seventeen governors, three national poet laurates, and Daniel Boone and Rebecca, of course."

They have completed their tour, letting Jordan inspect all the available sites and are concluding their rounds at the overlook that draws every visitor's attention.

"Heroes and rankers of every war this nation has ever fought, before and after it was a nation; a Vice President of these United States; writers, artists, merchants and tradesmen; farmers, preachers. And Presly O'Bannon. They're all here. There is more history in this cemetery than in any spot in the Commonwealth."

Goodman pauses for breath, and Jordan takes the opportunity. "I know. I grew up here," which stops Goodman and he looks in surprise at Jordan. They've just reached the monument and the view from it, with the town spread out before them and the Capitol dome poking through trees on its little hill on the other side of the valley, catches them both. It catches everyone.

Goodman is the first to recover.

"Of course," he says, "I should have known. Jordan Aimes. The writer. How did I not make that connection? Oh, the name on my appointment book. It was merely Mr. Aimes. No Jordan." He's embarrassed but smiling. "You will make a fine addition."

Which causes Jordan to laugh.

Jordan turns to scan the headstones along the path they've followed and up the little rise behind them—markers of stone in orderly rows among the towering oaks and stately maples in respectful attestation to the life remembered, some so old the lettering is blurred, some so new they glow when the sun strikes through the canopy of trees.

Jordan finishes his scan and turns back to Goodman, nodding, "Well, I'll be in good company. The men and women who made this town are here. Can't imagine better."

"So you've chosen your spot, then?"

And Jordan replies, with satisfaction in his voice, "I have."

You already know that the cemetery is beautiful. But beauty of its kind cannot be described.

It can be pictured.

Gene Burch has done a masterful job of this in a book he and Russ Hatter and Nicky Hughes have published, titled simply Frankfort Cemetery.

But photography can't, just as words can't, truly describe it.

To know the beauty of this place, it must be felt. The play of light and shadow on the headstones, the bird song and wind whisper in the breeze, the glint of sun on grass, the scent of the season in the air—redbud and dogwood blooming, fall leaves blanketing the ground—the absolute, encompassing peace beneath these ancient oaks and pines, this has to be felt.

Jordan's choice is Lot 119-R, #1-2, in Section M.

Section M is almost in the center of the cemetery, which is like a large elongated ellipse running along the ridge above the valley. Lot 119-R has a long, pleasing view down a vista of trees and grass and geometric rows of headstones with flowers around them. It is open to the sky, but with its own big oak just a few yards above where his right shoulder will be that will provide shade and songbirds among the leaves, and perhaps the call of owls out hunting in the dark.

And, for this was most important to him, it is among people he knows, or knows of, and not on the lone prairie.

The Boone monument is just up a little rise. The artist Paul Sawyier is close by. The solider poet Theodore O'Hara is across the road in the section dedicated to the Kentucky men and boys who gave their lives to duty and honor in the many wars they've been called on to fight.

Bruce is further up the road in Section T. Jesse is in Arlington.

It will do quite nicely, thank you.

They return to Goodman's office by the entry gate. Jordan signs the papers, writes the check, gets the Certificate of Ownership and they congratulate each other. He's bought a piece of ground. A real estate transaction. In a way he is disappointed. He had thought something more memorable would be the case. Something more formal, more ritualized. We're talking about eternity here. He shrugs. The important thing is that he leaves with his mind at ease about where he will lie when that times comes.

Now, two more bases to cover then ... Show-Time!

Since the day the boy from Brazil came calling and took him to that lonely grave on the abandoned farm near Peaks Mill, Jordan has been intrigued by the mystery of Honest Dick Tate.

It creeps into his mind at the oddest times and he finds himself thinking about it when he should be thinking about more important, and certainly more urgent, matters. So intrigued is he that he has to least know if there is enough to it that it might actually be the story it seems to be—the story that can't be passed up. Who better than the man who put the thought in his mind to begin with.

The afternoon is still young enough that Russ Hatter is in his office on the second floor of the Capital City Museum several blocks east of the Old Capitol grounds. He is the town's go-to historian and bard—the keeper of the flame. No man has a more encyclopedic knowledge of the history of the town or more passion for it. No one knows more about its heroes and villains, or takes more delight in the sharing their stories. He helped Jordan with a story once. They found they shared a fine appreciation for Eagle Rare, good books, and rambling conversations.

A rickety elevator gets you to his office. Books line its walls. Newspapers and maps and bundles of clippings fill the room. His desk is in the center of it all, with him behind it, poring intently over a map spread out across it.

"Well, as I live and breathe, the real Jordan Aimes," Hatter says, looking up to identify the intruder as Jordan comes through the door. Motioning to a book-stacked chair beside his desk, "clear that stuff away and take a seat and tell me all about what you're up to."

Hatter listened without interruption as Jordan told him of the boy from Brazil, of his visit to the grave, of the entreaty to come to Brazil and satisfy himself with the facts about the life of Honest Dick Tate and the kind of man he was; listened first with skepticism and then with fascination, and now is examining it all slowly in his mind and matching it with, and against, what he knows to be true and what he suspects might be.

"Tate is buried here? He's come home? Unbelievable. After all these years of mystery and supposition, we can finally know the full story—how he did it, why he did it, how he managed to stay hidden all those years, how and where he ended up? Answer all the questions? All you have to do is go to Brazil?"

"Tate walked off with close to nine million dollars in today's money—the biggest theft in Kentucky history. Drained the state treasury. The biggest outright theft in the whole country that year. And disappeared. Just totally vanished. Walked out of his office one sunny afternoon carrying two tobacco sacks full of cash, apparently to be deposited, told his staff he was on his way to Louisville and would be back in a week or so. And just disappeared.

"No one knows what happened to him. Or to the money. The search for him was international. There were reports that he had been seen in China, in Canada, in Brazil … in Kansas of all places. How did he do it? How did he evade all those people looking for him—the people hoping to claim the reward the state had posted, the journalists hungry for the story, the big- and small-time criminals hoping to find him and take the treasure for themselves? How did he hide all that money? Nine million dollars ain't no carrying-'round change.

"It's one of the most successful disappearances in history. Just a country boy. Born and raised out in the Peaks Mill area. His father a farmer. His mother a preacher's daughter. Bought up right. Churchgoing. Obeyed the Commandments. Straight as an arrow. He had only a high school education, but he must have had the most appealing personality ever honed. People loved him. They trusted him completely. Honest beyond doubt. Rock solid. Count on him.

"The people of Kentucky elected him State Treasurer and then proceeded to re-elect him every two years for the next twenty years. That's how much they loved and trusted him.

"He had a family, was a devoted family man. A wife. A daughter. Doted on them. They never saw him again. They got a few letters. How much he missed them. How sorry he was. How people misunderstood what had happened. Wished he was with them. Wished he could see them. How sad he was. How unhappy he was.

"He was just forty-seven. A life alone on the run with nine million dollars in tow. Dodging police. Dodging jackals. Never seen or heard from again."

"My God, you've got a crack at this story and you're hesitating?"

Ah, damn, Jordan thinks. I don't have time for this.

THURSDAY, OCTOBER 4
Day Twenty-Seven

A fine, fair day in the Bluegrass. Temperature in the low eighties, clear skies, a light breeze, the moon is waxing crescent.

Sunshine on the countryside. Birdsong in the air.

The Kavanaugh Supreme Court confirmation hearings are coming to an end in Washington.

The confirmed dead in the Sulawesi earthquake and tsunami: one-thousand four-hundred and seventy, so far.

National Boyfriend Day is today.

And Jordan is on the cusp of the decision.

To review the bidding:

Jordan Aimes is a white American male, age 48. Other than the inoperable aneurism that Danny (Dr. Daniel Moran, head of the Department of Neurosurgery at the University of San Francisco Medical Center) has discovered hiding in his brain, Jordan is in excellent health. He is comfortably successful, doing work he loves at which he is skilled, is vigorous and engaging, is in a satisfying relationship with a handsome and intelligent woman, is respected by his peers, and quite enjoying life.

He absolutely does not want it to end.

Jordan is not exactly sure why he is in this little river town in the Bluegrass of Kentucky. He was sure when he arrived—run to sanctuary when the threat is mortal.

The name should be Frank's Ford, anyway, not Frankfort.

Or Leestown.

Leestown is where all the action was. It was just a mile further downriver and was the more vibrant place until General James Wilkinson, hero of the Revolution, confidant of General George Washington, got his land grant and began promoting a tract near one of the safest fords on the Kentucky river just off the mouth of Benson Creek where poor Stephen Frank got killed—the tract on which the town of Frankfort grew.

Stephen Frank was one of a party of hunters on its way to Big Salt Lick to make salt for their little community of Bryant's Station.

The group camped for the night near that ford.

Just before dawn, Indians attacked, probably Cherokee or Shawnee. Frank was killed in the fight.

There is no written record. Did he die a hero, overwhelmed by screaming attackers, tomahawks flailing and arrows flying; fighting bravely and saving his companions?

He must have. His companions would not have named the place in his honor. Frank's Ford, they called it. They would not have done that for someone they cared little for, someone faint-hearted.

Afterwards, as people settled on Wilkinson's land and a village began to grow there, the name Frank's Ford segued into Frankfort.

Jordan tries to imagine how "Frank's Ford" became "Frankfort." Say it rapidly, slide the words together, hear it indistinctly. Franksford. Frankfort? Said that way often enough, heard that way often enough… yes, probably.

Stephen Frank must have been a hero. There should be a monument, or a small plaque at least, to note the event and honor him. Jordan is not aware of one.

History must be full of such slights. Jordan wonders what he has done that he will be remembered for. And will not want to be.

One last door to open. Aunt Maggie's. His mother's sister, her best friend.

Jordan is his mother's second child. Her first died in her arms, a boy not quite two months old. Pneumonia. She was nineteen.

She went a little crazy for a while but, thank God, Maggie was there. Maggie folded around her and she righted.

Jordan was born a year later. Fears that she might lose this baby, too, almost paralyzed her. But Maggie was there to calm her.

And he was there to hold on to.

When the dreads came, she would take him in her arms and hold him tight and whisper endearments in his ear as he snuggled close and sing softly to him. His warmth, his strong little body against hers, the smell of him, Ivory-soap-clean and baby-powder-sweet, was her comfort.

Him she would not lose.

Him she would love and protect and treasure and he would grow into a fine man that everyone would admire and in whom she would take inordinate pride.

She would have it no other way.

She and Maggie.

They were only a year or so apart. Maggie was the eldest.

Maggie was the pragmatic one, even from that early age. She saw things as they were and was comforting and cheerful whatever the circumstance. When things were to be faced, she faced them.

Maggie has a son of her own, John Edward, two years older than Jordan, off now in Cincinnati, an executive with the big consumer products company there. Jordan and John Edward spent a lot of time together as boys. She treated them like brothers. Lots of love. Not too many rules, but rigid ones to which they were held. Applause when they deserved it. Comfort when they needed it. And always a presence. She was there for them. Whenever, whatever. Understanding. Comforting. But firm. Actions have consequences. You do not dance around them.

Since his mother's death nine years ago, when Jordan has come through Frankfort on one of his trips in search of stories, the home he has come to for family is his Aunt Maggie's, today's destination.

He has only one question to ask her—to him, perhaps the most important one. He will not tell her of his condition. He knows the distress it will cause her, however bravely she takes it, and he does not want her answer to be conditioned on anything but the hard rock of honesty she has always shown.

Maggie is retired now. Forty-two years at Peaks Mill teaching freshman algebra and directing the school chorus. She took the job straight out of college and never regretted it. Her husband, Jake, owns the hardware and farm supply store at the Forks. He's still working, unlikely to stop until the doctors make him. Nothing to do with money. He's done very well over the years. He just can't imagine doing anything else ... except sometimes sitting in with Cal. Jake is a marvel with a banjo.

Their house at the Forks is the unofficial gathering place for the Macklins.

Maggie isn't the oldest of Jordan's Macklin aunts but has somehow, over the years, and not of her intention, become the doyenne. A testament, he supposes, to her warm disposition and the air of authority that drapes her like a cloak.

Jordan is expected for lunch. She has made his favorite, Hunter's Stew, and they are finishing up on the big back porch overlooking the lawn leading down to the creek. Sunny and warm, just the two of them. There has been the usual small talk, the catching up and the remembering. Aunt Maggie has been delighted with his presence and he has been luxuriating in her affection.

"Can you stay a while this time? Everyone would love to see you. We haven't had a family reunion in ages. You'd be the perfect reason. Next week? Here on the creek? Jake will set up the barbecues and the women will bring their favorite dishes. We'll arrange some tables out under the trees. Cal will bring his band. Can you?"

"Ah, Lord, Aunt Maggie, I'd love to. But I can't. I have this thing I have to do. I'll have to leave tomorrow or the next day."

"What is it, son?"

"Nothing to bother you with. But there is something I need to know before I do it."

"You want my burgoo recipe," she says laughing.

He smiles back, "No ma'am. It's this. You and mom put so much effort into me, so much love, so much understanding. You showed so much confidence in me, seemed so sure I'd make you proud—have I disappointed you? Have I turned out the way you hoped?"

"Jordy, what a strange question."

She reaches across the table and takes his hand.

"You've turned out just fine, son. Just fine. What's gotten into you? You were never fretful. What's bothering you?"

"What do you think happens next?"

"Next?"

"When I die. What happens then?"

"Why, you go to Heaven, son."

She seals this with a hug and a kiss, and a smile of reassurance that he remembers from his boyhood. It warms him.

They've parted now, he leaving with a jam cake wrapped in a bourbon cloth to keep it moist, and she with his promise he will quit thinking such ridiculous thoughts, but him thinking, even as unlikely as it seems to him, is this what he came for, for assurance?

Jordan has never had uncertainties about his ability to do whatever he sets his mind to. His self-confidence sometimes borders on arrogance. Yet somewhere deep in his hidden mind there is a little person still afraid of the dark, a small boy all alone and needing solace? He is needy and doesn't know it?

As for the other, the what-happens-next, he didn't mean to ask her that. He knew what her answer would be before he asked. A line from a poem slips into his mind. Stephen Vincent Benét. The world is ending and people are talking about what will happen at Judgment Day, and they're thinking he's a good fellow, it will be all right. Then the clouds part and they see "God's quiet face. Serenely merciless."

The thought gives him pause. But only for a moment.

He feels so good, so relieved at what his aunt had to say about him that he is willing to accept that a small boy might still be hiding somewhere in the closet of his mind, and he is not surprised that Billy's God might not be inclined to overlook disobedience.

FRIDAY, OCTOBER 5
Day Twenty-Eight

If Dr. Daniel Andrew Moran, Chief of Neurosurgery at the University of San Francisco Medical Center (Jordan prefers to think of it this way, with Danny's formal title and the world-class institution identified ... carries more authority then just Danny)—if the good doctor is right, the curtain will come crashing down any time now.

What if he's is wrong?

He is right, of course. All that science. All that knowledge. All those tests. All those experts examining and concurring—the good doctor has to be right.

But what if he isn't?

Jordan remembers times when Danny was wrong. Calling that pass in the flat when it was fourth-and-one on Shelbyville's goal-line. They would have won the title. All they needed was a yard. They'd been blowing the Devils left guard away all night. A yard. A simple quarterback sneak. Danny's call. Piece of cake. He calls the pass instead.

Or that night in the Cumberland coming back from fishing and the storm hits and the sleet starts and Danny is dead certain the left fork is the road to take when they get to the crossroad and he's wrong and the road dead-ends in a little stream at the bottom of a ravine and by then the sleet has turned to snow and they get stuck trying to turn around and they spend the night in the truck in the muck, freezing and hungry.

The dregs of the dream are still in his mind as he wakes, morning not yet come, rain against the window.

He can't call it back exactly. He needed to get to a place but couldn't. He was being menaced and had no weapon with which to defend himself.

As he struggles to get the dream clear in his mind, and still in the half fog of waking up, the menace segues into the blob in his brain, and the thought rises ... maybe Danny's wrong.

He likes that thought.

And drops back to sleep cuddling it warmly.

The rain has gone and the morning bright when he comes fully awake. He doesn't recall the dream, but he recalls the thought. It feels good to him. He enjoys the feeling through the morning ritual of getting ready for the day, but the glow begins to fade over the second cup of coffee, and he laughs, and shakes his head at himself—you're grasping at straws, ole buddy, sunk in wishful thinking. Danny is not wrong. The aneurism will burst. Just a matter of when.

But Jordan finds that thinking it won't burst and he'll still be good to go very comforting.

And then there's the matter of whether Danny can pull the operation off successfully.

There isn't a halfway decent bet in the whole lot.

If he is going to take Danny's option he must decide today. Tomorrow at the latest.

What doesn't he know that he needs to know? What is it that he lost or left here, that he forgot or never knew? That's why he's here, the Colonel said. He needs these answers before he can decide.

Something he left or lost?

He left his youth here. But he took the joy and the pain of it with him and it enriched him.

He lost his innocence. Things that he had been taught were true he found to be fictions as he grew and began to question. That the good guys don't always win may have been the most dismaying. That made him stronger, though. He lost his innocence in a more personal way, as well. But that was a discovery he savors still.

What had he forgotten?

How comforting those Sunday mornings in the little church surrounded by caring people could be and how good that made him feel. Billy made him remember that. And remembering made him realize how much he missed it. He cannot accept Billy's certainties or sit in his church masquerading as a believer, but he can decide what he can believe and believe that, and be true to his own little faith and not feel hypocritical if he slips into one of their services now and then just for the sheer comfort of it all.

So what's it gonna be, Jordy ole boy?

You've seen the people you wanted to see, got answers to the questions you thought you ought to ask. You've fished the water you wanted to fish, walked the town as it came awake. You've watched the stars make their transit while it slept, and the river turn to silver as the full moon rose. You've conjured up yesterdays and have a place to lay yourself down when the time comes to go.

That something you never knew? You always knew it, but didn't know you did. The only thing that really matters is how you feel about yourself.

Well, how do you? Are you a keeper?

You're at the top of your game. You're successful. You're respected by your peers. You're happy in your work, have a wide range of friends, eclectic interests, all your hair, and no belly. You can bench press your weight and wade fast water. You're not as bad as you might have been, or as good as you might could be, but give or take a few stumbles, you've acquitted yourself honorably and conducted yourself responsibly. All things considered, then, and allowing for prejudice, you'll do, Mr. Aimes, you'll do.

So there's your answer.

Get off the dime.

Decide!

There will be people to tell—the few who know your condition.

You've been successful in holding that confidential. The Colonel, Uncle Cal, Billy, Tom, they're the only ones you've told. None of the others know. Not Cindy. Not even Aunt Maggie or Hatter. No reason to burden them with the worry. When it's over, all they'll know is that Jordan came to visit and they had a nice time.

Liddy first.

Then Danny.

Well, to be certain, better tell yourself first.

Get it absolutely clear and mortally cemented in your own mind so that there is no going back on it.

No!

WEDNESDAY, OCTOBER 24
Day Forty-Seven

The Wyoming sky is so vast and cloudless he thinks he could see forever if only the light would last.

In the twilight, the river surface is as flat as glass. In this whole great sweep of land and sky there is only Jordan—a solitary fisherman making graceful casts trying for one last strike before dark.

From the deck of the lodge, Liddy is watching.

When he told her his decision, she knew for certain he would die. Tomorrow, the next day, a week at the latest.

Her anger was almost as intense as her sorrow. Jordan, Jordan, take the chance at least. Danny knows. The thing will burst. Let him try to save you.

But it was unarguable, not debatable, not even in the realm of rationality.

He had considered the evidence, had the procedure explained and demonstrated for him, understood the risks, weighed the odds to his own satisfaction, all the while realizing it was his life that was at stake. And he had decided, No.

He had listened patiently to her and had agreed that if anyone could pull of this feat of surgical wizardry, Dr. Daniel Moran and his team were the most likely.

It wasn't that he was afraid of death, she was sure of that, but he was unwilling to risk that the surgery might fail and leave him a vegetable for what was left of the rest of his life rather than kill him outright. He could not accept that.

If he had to gamble, Jordan preferred to gamble that there is an entity beyond our comprehension and understanding, a God, if that word helps, who set the universe in motion and, in the process of ordering the orbit of the planets and the blooming of the rose, also set the day we are to be born and the day we are to die—a minor detail in the assembling of infinity, but a date certain nevertheless.

Jordan believes his day has not yet arrived. He has the happy suspicion it may not arrive for quite some time.

So, he will play the hand he's holding.

He is either right, or lucky, for that was fourteen days ago and he is still among us, hale and hearty, chasing rainbows and browns on the bounteous North Platte and introducing Liddy to the delights of a proper mend to start a drag-free drift. He is happy, not apprehensive in the least, and eager for whatever the future holds, however much of it there is.

It would be serendipitous if Liddy were to turn out to be a natural. She won't. She is much more adept at fashioning a golf shot than shaping a graceful cast, but she is Game, and interested, and, with apologies for the pun, absolutely hooked by excitement when a keeper rainbow strikes her drifting midge. They won't be fishing partners. She hasn't the patience for it, or finds the satisfaction in solitude that he does. But as their time together on the North Platte is proving, they may well become partners in something more encompassing.

This recent experience has caused Jordan to begin to think in those terms. But he must be circumspect. Lydia Baccaro is as free a spirit as he is, with her own career and her own aspirations, just as successful in her field as he is in his, just as happy in her own special world as he is in his.

Could they meld those worlds into something that delighted them both? Should they try? He wonders.

But, ah, it is so pleasant in her company. And they do seem to fit each other so very well.

He had flown to San Francisco the morning after decision day—a short hop up to Dulles, a United nonstop from there to SFO.

The time zones in his favor, he was on the ground and in his place in the Oakland hills before dark. Dinner with Liddy. He needed to be in her reach when he told her so that she would have the chance to say her say to his face. He knows she thinks Danny's solution is the best of his options and she needs to be able to say that to him directly. And he knows she needs to understand why he's choosing the path he is taking. Only in each other's presence can that happen.

That done, then Danny in the morning, in his office on Parnassus Heights, with hope that Apollo and Dionysus would both be there to help him through it.

Danny has almost as much emotion invested in this as Jordan does. They were boys together, grew up together, have been fast friends all their lives. He would be as protective of Jordan's life as of his own. Only because as he saw it as the only chance for Jordan would he have offered the surgery. Only out of friendship would he have been willing to run the risk of failure and the bag of guilt he'd have to shoulder should Jordan die at his hands.

It was with relief that he listened as Jordan told him of his decision. All he said was, "I hope you're right, Jordy. I will never have been so happy to be wrong."

They had come to the lodge on the North Platte a week ago, he and Liddy.

Jordan wanted to resume the trip Danny's phone call had interrupted, and Liddy wanted to come, too. Whether she really wanted the experience or wanted to make sure she was at hand should it turn out that Danny was right and the aneurism burst and he drop dead then and there, he wasn't sure and he really didn't care. He was delighted with her company and they were growing closer.

Full moon tonight, the full moon of October, the Hunter's Moon. Good vibes it gives. A sign of good fortune, good hunting, fruitful times. The prairie will be as brightly lit as if at day.

They'll take their nightcap on the deck, watch the North Star rise and Orion stride the horizon. Then bed. Windows open, breeze just cool enough to make the blanket right, warmth against warmth, the scent of sage and the sound of night birds talking. No need to dream. This is Xanadu enough for now.

Tomorrow to São Paulo.

The story is aching to be told.

About the Author

Ron Rhody (Ronald E.) was a reporter, a sportswriter, and a broadcast journalist before segueing into a career as a corporate public relations executive.

He spent most of his corporate career directing the public relations and advertising programs of two of the country's largest corporations.

Now he is concentrating on writing and on perfecting his drag free-drifts He and his wife Patsy live in Pinehurst, North Carolina. He is a native Kentuckian. This is his fifth novel. All of them are set there., including this one.

Also by Ron Rhody

Fiction

THEO's Story

THEO & The Mouthful of Ashes

When THEO Came Home

Concerning the Matter of The King of Craw

Nonfiction

Our Own Little Fictions

Soccer: A Spectators Guide

The CEO's Playbook

Wordsmithing

All are available on Amazon.com and in fine bookstores everywhere.

Visit the author's website to learn more at

https://www.ronrhody.com/